"Shall I tell him to go away again and leave us alone for a couple of hours?" Amer said softly.

"I don't know what you mean." Leonora spoke with difficulty.

He was so close she could feel his little puffed breath of frustration. She thought, why doesn't he touch me? But still he did not.

Instead, he murmured, "That's the first lie you've ever told me," and she felt a sort of agony at his words.

She held her breath. But Amer rolled aside and sat up. He gave the boatman a few orders. He did not sound annoyed. He did not sound as if he cared much at all.

Leonora smoothed her hair with a shaking hand. She had never been so intensely aware of sensation before, nor of her own sensuality. Never realized so totally that she was a physical creature. Never *wanted....*

Dear Reader,

Let your imagination take flight as Sophie Weston brings you a truly delicious touch of Eastern promise.

Amer el-Barbary is an Arab prince, a true lord of the desert—every woman's fantasy man. He's rich and masterful, living life on the edge of danger. And he's about to capture Leonora Groom's heart—and your own—in this most romantic of stories, *The Sheikh's Bride*.

Look out next month in Harlequin Romance® for Lucy Gordon's *The Sheikh's Reward*

THE SHEIKH'S BRIDE

Sophie Weston

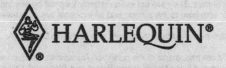

HARLEQUIN®

TORONTO • NEW YORK • LONDON
AMSTERDAM • PARIS • SYDNEY • HAMBURG
STOCKHOLM • ATHENS • TOKYO • MILAN • MADRID
PRAGUE • WARSAW • BUDAPEST • AUCKLAND

ISBN 0-373-03630-2

THE SHEIKH'S BRIDE

First North American Publication 2000.

PROLOGUE

'WHAT are we waiting for?' asked the co-pilot.

The pilot looked down from his cockpit at the Cairo tarmac. In the early morning, the dust was tinged with diamond light and the roofs of the distant airport building gleamed. A couple of men in dark suits were doing an efficient sweep of the apron on which their plane had come to a halt.

'Security,' he said briefly.

The co-pilot was new to flying the Sheikh of Dalmun's private fleet. 'Do they always go through this?'

The other man shrugged. 'He's an influential guy.'

'Is he a target, then?'

'He's megarich and he's heir apparent to Dalmun,' said the pilot cynically. 'Of course he's a target.'

His companion grinned. His girl-friend regularly brought home royalty watching magazines.

'Chick magnet, huh? Lucky devil.'

The security men had finished their surveillance. One of them raised a hand and a white stretch limousine came slowly round the plane. The pilot, his cap under his arm, stood up and went to shake hands with the departing passenger.

An early-morning breeze whipped the Sheikh's white robes as he strode towards the limousine. In spite of the entourage that followed, he looked a lonely figure.

The pilot came back into the cockpit.

'We're on stand-by,' he said briefly.

Other cars arrived. The security team swung into them then the limousine drew away, flanked by its guardians.

The pilots sat back, waiting for an escort to the plane's final parking place.

'What's he doing here?' asked the co-pilot idly. 'Business or pleasure?'

'Both, I guess. He hasn't been out of Dalmun for months,' said the older man unguardedly.

'Why?'

The pilot didn't answer.

'I heard there was a bust up. His old man wanted him to marry again?'

'Maybe.' A second monosyllabic answer.

'So what do you think? Has he been let out to find himself a bride?'

The pilot was betrayed into indiscretion. 'Amer el-Barbary? A *bride*? When hell freezes over.'

CHAPTER ONE

LEONORA pushed a grubby hand through her hair and breathed hard. The lobby of the Nile Hilton was full to bursting. She had lost three of the museum party she was supposed to be escorting; she had not managed to spend time with her mother who was consequently furious; and now this week's problem client had come up with another of her challenging questions.

'What?' she said distractedly.

'Just coming in now.' Mrs Silverstein nodded at the swing doors. 'Who *is* he?'

A stretched white limousine, its windows discreetly darkened, had pulled up in the forecourt, flanked by two dark Mercedes. Men in dark grey suits emerged and took up strategic stances while a froth of porters converged on the party. The doors of the limousine remained resolutely closed. Leo knew the signs.

'Probably royal.' She was not very interested. Her father's recently acquired travel agency did not have royal clients yet. 'Nothing to do with me, thank God. Have you seen the Harris family?'

'*Royal,*' said Mrs Silverstein, oblivious.

Leo grinned. She liked Mrs Silverstein.

'A lord of the desert,' the older woman said.

'Quite possibly.'

Leo decided not to spoil it by telling her the man was probably also Harvard educated, multilingual and rode through the desert in an air-conditioned four-wheel drive instead of on a camel. Mrs Silverstein was a romantic. Leo, as she was all too aware, was not.

'I wonder who he is…'

7

Leo knew that note in her voice. 'I haven't the faintest idea,' she said firmly.

Mrs Silverstein sent her a naughty look. 'You could ask.'

Leo laughed aloud. It was what her client had been saying to her for three weeks.

'Listen,' she said, 'I'm your courier. I'll do a lot for you. I'll ask women how old they are and men how much it costs to feed a donkey. But I won't ask a lot of armed goons who it is they're guarding. They'd probably arrest me.'

Mrs Silverstein chuckled. In three weeks they had come to understand each other. 'Chicken.'

'Anyway, I've got to find the Harris family.'

Leo slid through the crowd to a marble-topped table where a house phone lurked behind a formal flower arrangement. She dialled the Harris' room, casting a harassed eye round, just in case they had come down without her catching them.

The limousine party were on the move, she saw. Men, their mobile phones pressed to their ears, parted bodies. Behind them walked a tall figure, his robes flowing from broad shoulders. Mrs Silverstein was right, she thought ruefully. He was magnificent.

And then he turned his head and looked at her. And, to her own astonishment, Leo found herself transfixed.

'Hello?' said Mary Harris on the other end of the phone. 'Hello?'

She had never seen him before. Leo knew she had not. But there was something about the man that hit her like a high wind. As if he was important to her. As if she *knew* him.

'Hello? Hello?'

He wore the pristine white robe and headdress of a desert Arab. In that glittering lobby the severe plainness was a shock. It made him look even more commanding than he already did given his height and the busy vigilance of his entourage. His eyes were hidden by dark glasses but his expression was weary as his indifferent glance slid over her and on across the crowd.

'Hello? Who is this?'

Leo read arrogance in every line of him. She did not like it. But still she could not stop staring. It was like being under a spell.

Mrs Silverstein slid up beside her and took the phone out of her hand. Leo hardly noticed. All she could do was look—and wait for his eyes to find her again.

I'm not like this, said a small voice in her head. *I don't stare blatantly at sexy strangers.* Leo ignored it. She did not seem as if she could help herself. She stood as still as a statue, *waiting*...

A man Leo recognised as the hotel's duty manager was escorting the party. He was bowing, oblivious to anyone else. As he did so, he brushed so close to her that she had to step back sharply. She hit her hip on the table and grabbed a pillar to save herself. Normally a gentle and courteous man, the duty manager did not even notice.

But the object of all this attention did.

The white-robed figure stopped dead. Masked eyes turned in Leo's direction.

It was what she had been waiting for. It was like walking into an earthquake. Leo's breath caught and she hung onto the pillar as if she would be swallowed up without its support.

'Oh my,' said Mrs Silverstein, fluttering.

Leo clutched even tighter. She felt cold—then searingly hot—then insubstantial as smoke. Her fingers on the pillar were white but she felt as if the strength had all been slammed out of her.

Then he turned his head away. She was released.

Leo sagged. She found she had been holding her breath and her muscles felt as weak as water. She put a shaky hand to her throat.

'Oh *my*,' said Mrs Silverstein a second time. She gave Leo a shrewd look and restored the phone to its place.

Across the lobby, there was an imperious gesture. One of the suited men stepped respectfully close. The tall head inclined. The assistant looked across at Mrs Silverstein and Leo. He seemed surprised.

Leo knew that surprise. The knowledge chilled her, just as it had in every party she had ever been to. She was not the sort of woman that men noticed in crowded lobbies. She and the man in the grey suit both knew it.

She was too tall, too pale, too stiff. She had her father's thick eye brows. They always made her look fierce unless she was very careful. Just now, too, her soft dark hair was full of Cairo dust and her drab business suit was creased.

Not very enticing, Leo thought, trying to laugh at herself. She had got used to being plain. She would have said that she did not let it bother her any more. But the look of surprise on the man's face hurt surprisingly.

The white-robed figure said something sharply. His assistant's face went blank. Then he nodded. And came over to them.

'Excuse me,' he said in accentless English. 'His Excellency asks if you are hurt.'

Leo shook her head, dumbly. She was too shaken to speak—though she could not have said why. After all, with his eyes hidden by smoked glass, she had no evidence that the man in the white robes was even looking at her. But she knew he was.

Mrs Silverstein was made of sterner stuff.

'Why how kind of—of His Excellency to ask,' she said, beaming at the messenger. She turned to Leo, 'That man didn't hurt you, did he dear?'

'*Hurt* me?' echoed Leo. She was bewildered. Did he have laser-powered eyes behind those dark glasses?

Mrs Silverstein was patient. 'When he bumped into you.'

Leo remembered the small collision with the under manager.

'Oh. Mr Ahmed.'

She pulled herself together but it was an effort. The sheikh was no longer looking at her. Leo knew that without looking at him. She was as conscious of him as if her whole body had somehow been tuned to resonate to his personal vibration.

No one had ever done that to her before. *No one;* let alone a regal stranger whose eyes she could not read. It shocked her.

She swallowed and said as steadily as she could manage, 'No, of course not. It was nothing.'

Mrs Silverstein peered up at her. 'Are you sure? You look awful pale.'

The security man did not offer any view on Leo's pallor or otherwise. She had the distinct impression that this was not the first time he had carried a message to an unknown lady. But that the messages were normally more amusing and the ladies more sophisticated; and about a hundred times more glamorous.

'Can I offer you assistance of any kind, madam?'

Leo moistened her lips. But she pulled herself together and said more collectedly, 'No, thank you. It was nothing. I don't need any assistance.' She remembered her manners. 'Please thank His Excellency for his concern. But there was no need.'

She turned away. But Mrs Silverstein was not going to pass up the chance of a new experience so easily. Not when royalty was involved. She tapped the security man on the arm.

'Which Excellency is that?'

The security man was so taken aback that he answered her.

'Sheikh Amer el-Barbary.'

Mrs Silverstein was enchanted. 'Sheikh,' she echoed dreamily.

Just a few steps away the dark glasses turned in their direction again. Leo felt herself flush. She did not look at him but she could feel his sardonic regard as if someone had turned a jet of cold water on her.

She shivered. How does he do that? she thought, aware of the beginnings of indignation.

Uncharacteristically her chin came up. Leo was a peacemaker, not a fighter. But this time was different. She glared across the lobby straight at him, as if she knew she was meeting his eyes.

Was it her imagination, or did the robed figure still for a moment? Leo had the feeling that suddenly she had his full attention. And that he was not best pleased

Help, she thought. *He's coming over.* The hairs on the back of her neck rose.

And then rescue came from an unexpected quarter.

'Darling!' called a voice.

Leo jumped and looked wildly round. The lobby seethed with noisy groups talking in numerous languages. They were no competition for her mother. Years of ladies' luncheons had given Deborah Groom a vocal pitch that could cut steel.

'Darling,' she called again. 'Over here.'

A heavily ringed hand waved imperiously. Leo located it and counted to ten. She had tried to persuade her mother not to come to Cairo in the busiest week of the agency's year. Deborah, predictably, had taken no notice.

Now Leo pulled herself together and said briskly to the hovering security man, 'Thank you but I am quite all right. Please—' she allowed herself just a touch of irony which she was sure the man would miss '—reassure His Excellency.' Then, more gently to Mrs Silverstein, 'Give me ten minutes. I have to clear up a couple of things. Then, if you still want to go, I'll take you to the pyramids at Giza.'

'You go right ahead,' said Mrs Silverstein, still entranced by her brush with royalty. 'I'll go sit in the café and have a cappuccino. Come and find me when you're done.'

Leo gave her a grateful smile. Then she tucked her clipboard under her arm and swarmed professionally through the crowd.

'Hello, Mother,' she said, bending her tall head. Leo received the scented breath on the cheek which Deborah favoured with a kiss and straightened thankfully. 'Having a good time?'

Deborah Groom was known for going straight to the point. 'It would be better if I saw something of my only daughter.'

Leo kept her smile in place with an effort. 'I warned you I'd have to work.'

'Not all the time.'

'There's a lot on.' If she sounded absent it was because in the distance she could see Andy Francis trying to herd a group towards their waiting bus. He was not having much success but then he should not have been doing it alone. Roy Ormerod, the head of Adventures in Time, was scheduled to be with the party too.

Deborah frowned. 'Does your chief know who you are?'

Leo gave a crack of laughter. 'You mean does he know that I'm the boss's daughter? Of course not. That would defeat the whole object. I'm called Leo Roberts here.'

Deborah snorted. 'I just don't understand your father sometimes.'

That was nothing new. She had walked out on Gordon Groom fourteen years ago, saying exactly that and leaving him to care for the ten-year-old Leo.

'He thinks it's a good idea for me to learn to stand on my own feet like he did,' she said patiently. 'Look, Mother—'

'You mean he thinks if he turns you out in the world to cope on your own you'll turn into a boy,' Deborah snapped.

Leo's eyes flashed. But there was enough truth in the accusation to make her curb her instinct to retort in kind. She and her mother both knew that Gordon had always wanted a son. Training Leo to succeed him in the business was just second best. He did not even try to disguise that any more.

Deborah bit her lip. 'Oh, I'm sorry darling, I promised myself I wouldn't start that again,' she said remorsefully. 'But when I see you looking like death and running yourself ragged like this, I just can't help myself.'

'Forget it,' said Leo.

She cast a surreptitious look at her clipboard. Where was Roy? He should have paid the bus driver for the Japanese party. If he didn't turn up she would have to deal with it.

And what about the Harris family? She had forgotten all about them and the museum tour was leaving.

Her mother sighed. 'I suppose there's no hope of seeing you at all today?'

Leo's conscience smote her. 'Not a chance unless—'

Mary Harris panted up to her.

'Oh, Leo, I'm so sorry. Timothy got locked in the bathroom. I didn't know what to do. The room attendant got him out. Have we missed the tour?'

Leo reassured them and plugged them rapidly onto the departing group. She came back to Deborah, mentally reviewing her schedule.

'Look, Mother, there's one more group I've got to see on its way. And then I'm supposed to take someone to the pyramids. But it will be hot and she's quite elderly. I doubt if she'll want to stay too long. Tea this afternoon?'

Deborah perked up. 'Or could I give you dinner?'

Leo hesitated.

'You think your father wouldn't like it,' Deborah diagnosed. Her mouth drooped.

Leo almost patted her hand. But Deborah would have jumped a foot. They were not a touchy-feely family.

So she said gently, 'It's not that. There's a conference dinner. We've arranged it at an historic merchant's house and there's going to be a lot of bigwigs present. I really ought to be there.'

'If the wigs are that big, why can't your boss do it?' Deborah said shrewdly.

Leo gave a choke of laughter. 'Roy? He doesn't—'

But then she thought about it. The guest list included some of the most illustrious charitable foundations in the world, including a high royalty quotient. Roy liked mingling at parties where he had a good chance of being photographed with the rich and famous. He called it networking.

'Mother, you're a genius. It's just the thing for Roy,' she said. She pulled out her mobile phone.

All she got was his answering machine. Leo left a crisp message and rang off.

'Right, that's sorted. I'll see you tonight. Now I've got to take a seventy-year-old from New Jersey to Giza.'

Deborah muttered discontentedly.

Leo looked down at her.

'What?'

'Surely someone junior could take this woman to the pyramids?'

Leo grinned. Deborah had been a rich man's daughter when she married rising tycoon Gordon Groom. There had been someone junior to take care of tedious duties all her life. It was one of the reasons Gordon had fought so hard for the custody of his only child.

'As long as I'm a member of the team, I do my share of the chores,' she said equably.

'Sometimes you are so like your father,' Deborah grumbled.

Leo laughed. 'Thank you.'

Deborah ignored that. 'I don't know why he had to buy Adventures in Time, anyway. Why couldn't he stick to hotels? And civilised places? What does he want with a travel agency?'

'Diversify or die,' Leo said cheerfully. 'You know Pops—' She broke off. 'Whoops.'

In the Viennese café Mrs Silverstein was chatting to an alarmed-looking man in a grey suit. Leo was almost certain he was a member of Sheikh el-Barbary's entourage.

'It looks as if my client is getting bored. I'll pick you up at eight this evening, Mother.'

She darted into the crowd. It was a relief.

Deborah's divorce from Gordon Groom had been relatively amicable and her settlement kept her luxuriously provided for, but she could still be waspish about her workaholic ex-husband. It was the one subject that she and Leo were guaranteed to argue about every time they got together.

Tonight, Leo promised herself, she was not going to let

Deborah mention Gordon once. Leo was beginning to have her own misgivings about her father's plans for her. But she was going to keep that from Deborah until she was absolutely certain herself. So they would talk about clothes and make-up and boyfriends and all the things that Deborah complained that Leo wasn't interested in.

One fun evening, thought Leo wryly, after another wonderful day. She went to rescue the security man.

The Sheikh's party swept into the suite like an invading army. One security man went straight to the balcony. The other disappeared into the bedroom. The manager, bowing, started to demonstrate the room's luxurious facilities. He found the Sheikh was not listening.

An assistant, still clutching his brief-case and laptop computer, nodded gravely and backed the manager towards the door.

'Thank you,' said the Sheikh's assistant. 'And now the other rooms?'

The manager bowed again and led the way. The security men followed.

The Sheikh was left alone. He went out to the balcony and stood looking across the Nile. The river was sinuous and glittering as a lazy snake in the morning sun. There was a dhow in midstream, he saw. Its triangular sail was curved like scimitar. It looked like a small dark toy.

He closed his eyes briefly. It was against more than the glare reflected off the water. Why did everything look like toys, these days?

Even the people. Moustafa, his chief bodyguard, looked like a prototype security robot. And the woman he was seeing tonight. He intended quitting the boring conference dinner with an excuse he did not care if they believed or not in order to see her. But for an uncomfortable moment, he allowed himself to realise that she reminded him of nothing so much as a designer-dressed doll. In fact, all the women he had seen recently looked like that.

Except—he had a fleeting image of the girl who had tumbled against the pillar in the hotel lobby. She was too tall, of course. And badly turned out, with her hair full of dust and a dark suit that was half-way to a uniform. But uniform or not, she had not looked like a doll. Not with those wide, startled eyes. The sudden shock in them had been intense—and unmistakeably real.

The Sheikh's brows twitched together in a quick frown. Why had she looked so shocked? He suddenly, passionately, wanted to know. But of course he never would, now. He grunted bad temperedly.

His personal assistant came back into the suite. He hesitated in the doorway.

The Sheikh straightened his shoulders. 'Out here, Hari,' he called. There was resignation in his tone.

The assistant cautiously joined him on the balcony.

'Everything appears to be in order,' he reported.

The Sheikh took off his dark glasses. His eyes were amused but terribly weary.

'Sure? Have the guys checked thoroughly? No bugs in the telephone? No poison in the honey cakes?'

The assistant smiled. 'Moustafa can take his job too seriously,' he admitted. 'But better safe than sorry.'

His employer's expression was scathing. 'This is nonsense and we both know it.'

'The kidnappings have increased,' Hari pointed out in a neutral tone.

'At home,' said the Sheikh impatiently. 'They haven't got the money to track me round the world, poor devils. Anyway, they take prosperous foreign visitors who will pay ransom. Not a local like me. My father would not pay a penny to have me back.' He thought about it. 'Probably pay them to keep me.'

Hari bit back a smile. He had not been present at the interview between father and son before Amer left Dalmun this time. But the reverberations had shaken the city.

A terminal fight, said the palace. The father would never

speak to the son again. An ultimatum, said Amer's household; the son had told his father he would tolerate no more interference and was not coming back to Dalmun until the old Sheikh accepted it.

Amer eyed him. 'And you can stop looking like a stuffed camel. I know you know all about it.'

Hari disclaimed gracefully. 'I just hear the gossip in the bazaars, like everyone else,' he murmured.

Amer was sardonic. 'Good for business, is it?'

'Gossip brings a lot of traders into town, I'm told,' Hari agreed.

'Buy a kilo of rice and get the latest palace dirt thrown in.' Amer gave a short laugh. 'What are they saying?'

Hari ticked the rumours off on his fingers. 'Your father wants to kill you. You want to kill your father. You have refused to marry again. You are insisting on marrying again.' He stopped, his face solemn but his lively eyes dancing. 'You want to go to Hollywood and make a movie.'

'Good God.' Amer was genuinely startled. He let out a peal of delighted laughter. 'Where did that one come from?'

Hari was not only his personal assistant. He was also a genuine friend. He told him the truth. 'Cannes last year, I should think.'

'Ah,' said Amer, understanding at once. 'We are speaking of the delicious Catherine.'

'Or,' said Hari judiciously, 'the delicious Julie, Kim or Michelle.'

Amer laughed. 'I like Cannes.'

'That shows in the photographs,' Hari agreed.

'Disapproval, Hari?'

'Not up to me to approve or disapprove,' Hari said hastily. 'I just wonder—'

'I like women.'

Hari thought about Amer's adamant refusal to marry again after his wife was killed in that horse riding accident. He kept his inevitable reflections to himself.

'I like the crazy way their minds work,' Amer went on.

'It makes me laugh. I like the way they try to pretend they don't know when you're looking at them. I like the way they smell.'

Hari was surprised into pointing out, 'Not all women smell of silk and French perfume like your Julies and your Catherines.'

'Dolls,' said Amer obscurely.

'What?'

'Has it occurred to you how many animated dummies I know? Oh they *look* like people. They walk and talk and even sound like people. But when you talk to them they just say the things they've been programmed to say.'

Hari was unmoved. 'Presumably they're the things you want them to say. So who did the programming?'

Amer shifted his shoulders impatiently. 'Not me. I don't want—'

'To date a woman who has not been programmed to say you are wonderful?' Hari pursued ruthlessly. He regarded his friend with faint scorn. 'Why don't you try it, some time?'

Amer was not offended. But he was not impressed, either.

'Get real,' he said wearily.

Hari warmed to his idea. 'No, I mean it. Take that girl down stairs in the lobby just now.'

Amer was startled. 'Have you started mind reading, Hari?'

'I saw you looking her way,' Hari explained simply. 'I admit I was surprised. She's hardly your type.'

Amer gave a mock shudder. 'No French perfume there, you mean. I know. More like dust and cheap sun-tan lotion.' A reminiscent smile curved his handsome mouth suddenly. 'But even so, she has all the feminine tricks. Did you see her trying to pretend she didn't know I was looking at her?'

Hari was intrigued. 'So why were you?'

Amer hesitated, his eyes unreadable for an instant. Then he shrugged. 'Three months in Dalmun, I expect,' he said in his hardest voice. 'Show a starving man stale bread and he forgets he ever knew the taste of caviar.'

'Stale bread? Poor lady.'

'I'll remember caviar as soon as I have some to jog my memory,' Amer murmured mischievously.

Hari knew his boss. 'I'll book the hotel in Cannes.'

It was not a successful visit to the pyramids. As Leo expected, Mrs Silverstein insisted on walking round every pyramid and could not be persuaded to pass on the burial chamber of Cheops. Since that involved a steep climb, a good third of which had to be done in a crouching position, the older woman was in considerable pain by the end of the trip. Not that she would admit it.

Ever since Mrs Silverstein arrived in Egypt on her Adventures in Time tour, she had wanted to see everything and, in spite of her age and rheumatic joints, made a spirited attempt to do so. When other members of the group took to shaded rooms in the heat of the afternoon, Mrs Silverstein was out there looking at desert plants or rooting affronted Arabs out of their afternoon snooze to bargain over carpets or papyrus.

'The woman never *stops*,' Roy Ormerod complained, looking at the couriers' reports. 'She'll collapse and then we'll be responsible. For Heaven's sake get her to slow down.'

But Leo, joining one of the party's trips, found she had a sneaking sympathy for Mrs Silverstein. She was a lively and cultivated woman with a hunger for new experience that a lifetime of bringing up a family had denied her. She also, as Leo found late one night when the local courier thankfully surrendered her problem client and retired to bed, had a startling courage.

'Well, it's a bit more than rheumatism,' Mrs Silverstein admitted under the influence of honey cakes and mint tea. 'And it's going to get worse. I thought, I've got to do as much as I can while I can. So I'll have some things to remember.'

Leo was impressed. She said so.

'You see I always wanted to travel,' Mrs Silverstein confided. 'But Sidney was such a homebody. And then there were the children. When they all got married I thought *now*.

But then Sidney got sick. And first Alice was divorced and then Richard and the grandchildren would come and stay…' She sighed. 'When Dr Burnham told me what was wrong I thought—it's now or never, Pat.'

Leo could only admire her. So, instead of following Roy's instructions, she did her best to make sure that Mrs Silverstein visited every single thing she wanted to see in Egypt, just taking a little extra care of her. It was not easy.

By the time Leo got her back to the hotel she was breathing hard and had turned an alarming colour. Leo took her up to her room and stayed while Mrs Silverstein lay on the well-sprung bed, fighting for breath. Leo called room service and ordered a refreshing drink while she applied cool damp towels to Mrs Silverstein's pink forehead.

'I think I should call a doctor,' she said worriedly.

Mrs Silverstein shook her head. 'Pills,' she said. 'In my bag.'

Leo got them. Mrs Silverstein swallowed three and then lay back with her eyes closed. Her colour slowly returned to normal.

The phone rang. Leo picked it up.

'Mrs Silverstein?' said a harsh voice she knew all too well. Even when Roy Ormerod was trying to be conciliating he sounded angry. 'I wonder if you can tell me where Miss Roberts went when she left you?'

Leo braced herself. 'This is me, Roy. Mrs Silverstein wasn't feeling well, so I—'

He did not give her the chance to finish.

'What the hell do you think you're doing? I told you to stop that old bat going on excursions, not give her personal guided tours. You should be back at the office. And what do you mean, leaving me a message that you won't be at the dinner, tonight? You've got to be there. It's part of your job.…'

He ranted for several more minutes. Mrs Silverstein opened her eyes and began to look alarmed.

Leo interrupted him. 'We'll talk about this at the office,'

she said firmly. She looked at her watch. 'I'll come over now.
See you in half an hour.'

'No you won't. I'm already—'

But she had cut him off.

'Trouble?' said Mrs Silverstein.

'None I can't handle.'

'Is it my fault?'

'No,' said Leo.

Because it was not. Roy had been spoiling for a fight ever
since she first arrived from London.

Forgetting professional discretion, Leo said as much. Mrs
Silverstein looked thoughtful. She had met Roy.

'And he doesn't like it that you're not attracted to him,'
she said wisely.

Leo stared. 'What? Oh, surely not.'

Mrs Silverstein shrugged. 'Good at your job. Independent.
Clients like you. All sounds too much like competition to
me, honey.' She struggled up among the pillows. 'The only
way you could put yourself right with the man is by falling
at his feet.'

Leo stared, equally fascinated and repelled.

'I hope you're wrong,' she said with feeling.

There was a knock at the door. Leo got off the side of the
bed.

'That must be your lemon sherbet.'

But it was not. It was Roy. His eyes were bulging with
fury.

'Oh, you were calling from the desk,' said Leo, enlightened.

He brushed that aside. 'Look here—' he began loudly.

Leo barred his way, giving thanks for the carved screen
behind the tiny entrance area. It masked the doorway from
Mrs Silverstein's view.

'You can't make a scene here,' she hissed. 'She's not
well.'

But Roy was beyond rationality. He took Leo by the wrist

and pulled her out into the corridor. He was shouting. He even took her by the shoulders and shook her.

An authoritative voice said, 'That is enough.'

They both turned, Leo blindly, Roy with blundering aggression.

The speaker was a man with a haughty profile and an air of effortless command. A business man, Leo thought. Someone who had paid for expensive quiet on this executive floor and was going to see that he got what he paid for. The dark eyes resting on Roy were coldly contemptuous.

Roy did not like his intervention. 'Who are you? The floor manager?' he sneered.

Leo winced for him. On the face of it, the stranger's impeccable dark suit was indistinguishable from any of the other business suits in the hotel. But Leo's upbringing had taught her to distinguish at a glance between the prosperous and the seriously rich. The suit was hand tailored and, for all its conservative lines, individually designed as well. Add to that the air of being in charge of the world, and you clearly had someone to reckon with.

But Roy had never been able to read nonverbal signs.

He said pugnaciously, 'This is a private conversation.'

'Then you should conduct it in private,' the man said. His courtesy bit deeper than any invective would have done. 'You have a room here?'

'No,' said Leo, alarmed at the thought of being alone with Roy in this mood.

For the first time the man took his eyes off the belligerent Roy. He sent her a quick, cool look. And did a double take.

'Mademoiselle?' he said blankly.

Leo did not recognise him. She tried to pull herself together and search her memory. But Roy's shaking of her seemed to have scrambled her brains.

Meanwhile, the fact that the stranger seemed to recognise her had sent Roy into a frenzy.

'You want to be careful with that one, friend,' he said. 'She'll stab you in the back as soon as look at you.'

Leo's head spun as if she had been shot. All she could think of was that Roy must have found out who her father was.

'What?' she said hoarsely.

The stranger sent her a narrow-eyed look. 'It is perhaps that I intrude unnecessarily,' he said, his accent pronounced. 'Mademoiselle?'

Leo shook her confused head.

Roy snarled, 'You're fired.'

Leo paled. She could just imagine what her father would say to this news.

'Oh Lord,' she said with foreboding.

This time the stranger did not bother to look at her.

'Your discussion would benefit from a more constructive approach,' he told Roy austerely.

Roy snorted. 'Discussion over,' he snapped. He sent Leo one last flaming look. 'You don't want to come to the dinner tonight? Fine. Don't. And don't come near the office again, either. Or any of my staff.'

Leo began to be alarmed. She shared an apartment with two of his staff.

'Roy—'

But he was on a roll. 'And don't ask me for a reference.'

Leo was not as alarmed about that as he clearly thought she should have been. When she said, 'Look, let's talk about this,' in a soothing voice, two bright spots of colour appeared on Roy's cheeks.

He took a hasty step forward. Leo thought in a flash of recognition: He is going to hit me. It was so crazy she did not even duck. Instead she froze, panicking.

Fortunately their companion did not panic so easily. He stepped swiftly in front of her.

'No,' he said.

It was quiet enough but it had the force of a blow.

Leo winced. It stopped Roy dead in his tracks. For a moment he and her rescuer stood face-to-face, eyes locked. Roy was a big man and the red glare in his eyes was alarming.

The other was tall and his shoulders were broad enough but, under the exquisite tailoring, he was slim and graceful. No match for a bull like Roy, you would have said. Yet there was no doubt who was the master in this encounter.

There was a moment of tense silence. Roy breathed hard. Then, without another word, he turned and blundered off, sending a chair flying.

Leo sagged against the wall. Her heart was racing. Now that it was over she was horrified at the ugly little scene.

Out of sight, she heard the lift doors open...several people get out...voices. Her rescuer flicked a look down the corridor. The voices got louder, laughing. He slipped a hand under her arm.

'Come with me.'

And before the new arrivals caught sight of them, he had whisked her to the end of the corridor and through impressive double doors. Before she knew what was happening, Leo found herself sitting in a high-backed chair in what she recognised as the Presidential Suite. The man stood over her, silent. He looked half impatient; half—what? Leo felt her heart give a wholly unfamiliar lurch.

'Are you all right?' he said at last.

Leo thought: I want him to put his arms round me. She could not believe it.

'What?' she said distractedly.

He frowned. As if people usually paid closer attention when he spoke, Leo thought. Now she came to look at him closely she saw there was more to him than grace and good tailoring. The harsh face might be proud and distant but it was spectacularly handsome. And surely there was a look in those eyes that was not proud or distant at all?

I must be hallucinating, Leo thought feverishly. This is not my scene at all. I don't fancy chance-met strangers and they don't fancy me. This is the second time today I've started to behave like someone I don't know. Am I going mad?

'I said, are you all right?'

'Oh.' She tried to pull herself together. 'I—suppose so.' She added almost to herself, 'I just don't know what to do.'

He sighed heavily. 'In what way?' His distaste was obvious.

If he dislikes this situation so much, why doesn't he just leave me alone, Leo thought irritated.

'He said I wasn't to go back. But everything I have is at the flat…'

Unexpectedly her voice faltered. To her horror, Leo felt tears start. She dashed them away angrily. But the little gesture gave her away more completely than if she had started to bawl aloud.

The man's face became masklike.

'You live with this man?'

But Leo's brain was racing, proposing and discarding courses of action at the rate of ten a minute. She hardly noticed his question.

'I'll have to call London.' She looked at her watch. 'And then book a room somewhere. If I can get one in the height of the tourist season.'

The man sighed. 'Then it will be my pleasure to offer you my assistance,' he said in a long-suffering tone. He picked up the phone.

Leo's brows twitched together. There was something oddly familiar about the formal phrase.

'Have we met?'

He was talking into the phone in quick, clicking Arabic. But at that he looked down at her.

'We have not, Miss Roberts.'

He had the strangest eyes. She had thought they would be brown in that dark face but they were not. They were a strange metallic colour, somewhere between cold steel and the depths of the sea; and dark, dark. Leo felt herself caught by their icy intensity; caught and drawn in, under, drowned…

She pulled herself up short. Was the man a mesmerist?

'You know my name,' she pointed out breathlessly.

He smiled then. For the first time. It made him devastating.

'I can read.'

She stared at him, uncomprehending. He reached out a hand and brushed her shoulder. Even through the poplin jacket of her suit, his touch was electric. Leo shot to her feet with a gasp.

'What—?'

'Your label,' he said gently.

He had removed the large lettered name tag that she had worn to the airport this morning. He dropped it into her hand, not touching her fingers.

Leo's face heated. She felt a fool. That was not like her, either. *What is it about this man that makes me lose my rationality? And feel like I've never felt before?*

The phone rang. He picked it up, listened without expression and only the briefest word of acknowledgement before ringing off.

'The hotel has a room for you. Pick the key up at the desk.'

Leo was startled into protesting. 'A room? *Here?* You're joking. They're booked solid for weeks. I know because I was trying to get a room for a late attender at the conference.'

He shrugged, bored. 'One must have become available in the meantime.'

Leo did not believe that for a moment. Her eyes narrowed.

But before she could demand an explanation, the door banged back on its hinges and two large men in tight suits appeared at it. One of them was carrying a revolver. Leo gaped.

Her rescuer spun round and he said something succinct. The gun stopped pointing at her. The two men looked uncomfortable. Leo turned her attention from the new arrivals to her rescuer.

'Who *are* you?'

He hesitated infinitesimally. Then, 'My name is Amer,' he said smoothly.

Leo's suspicions increased. But before she could demand further information, one of the men spoke agitatedly. Her rescuer looked at his watch.

'I have to go,' he said to her. 'Moustafa will take you down to the lobby and ensure that there are no problems.'

He gave her a nod. It was sharp and final. He was already walking away before Leo pulled herself together enough to thank him. Which was just as well. Because she was not feeling grateful at all.

CHAPTER TWO

LEO was not really surprised when the room proved to be not only available but also quietly luxurious. When a discreetly noncommittal porter ushered her in she found there were gifts waiting on the brass coffee table: a bowl of fruit, a dish of Arabic sweetmeats and a huge basket of flowers.

Leo blinked. 'That's—very beautiful.'

The porter nodded without expression. He surrendered the plastic wafer that served as a key to her room and backed out. Neither he nor the hotel receptionist had expressed the slightest surprise about her lack of luggage.

It was unnerving. Leo felt as if the unknown stranger had cast some sort of magic cloak over her. Oh, it was protective all right. But it made her feel as if he had somehow made her invisible as well.

Still, at least it had got her a roof over her head tonight. Be grateful for small mercies, she told herself. He's given you the opportunity to get your life back on track. She checked her watch and started making phone calls.

Her mother was fourth on the list. She expected to have to leave a message but Deborah was there.

'Sorry, Mother, you're going to have to take a rain check for tonight,' she said. 'I've got problems. They'll take a bit of time to sort out.'

'Tell me,' said Deborah.

Leo did.

Her mother was indignant. She might not approve of her only daughter toiling as a menial courier but that did not mean that she thought anyone had the right to sack her. She urged various strategies on Leo, most of which would have ended with both Roy and Leo being deported. Used to her mother's fiery temperament, Leo murmured soothing noises down the phone until her mother's fury abated.

'Well,' said Deborah pugnaciously, 'Mr Ormerod is certainly not interrupting my dinner plans. You have to eat and I want your company. See you at eight o' clock.'

'But I haven't got anything to *wear*,' wailed Leo.

'You've got a credit card.' She could hear the glee in her mother's voice. Deborah was always complaining about Leo's lack of interest in clothes. 'And you ought to know this town well enough to know where the class boutiques are. I'll see you downstairs *now*.'

Leo knew when she was beaten. She negotiated a fifteen-minute delay to allow her to make the rest of her calls. But that was as much of a concession as Deborah was willing to make.

Deborah was waiting in the lobby.

'I've got a car,' she said briskly. 'And I know where to go, too, so don't try to fob me off with any old shopping mall.'

She led the way purposefully. Leo grinned and followed.

Installed in the back of the hired limousine, Leo tipped her head back and looked at her mother appreciatively. Deborah fluffed up the organza collar to her stunning navy-and-white designer dress. The discreet elegance of her earrings did not disguise the fact that they were platinum or that the navy stones which echoed her ensemble were rather fine sapphires.

'You look very expensive,' Leo said lazily.

She did not mean it as a criticism. But Deborah flushed. She swung round on the seat to inspect her weary daughter.

'And you look like a tramp,' she retorted. 'Do you dress like that to make a point?'

Leo was unoffended. She had been taller than her exquisite mother when she was eleven. By the time she entered her teens she had resigned herself to towering over other girls. She had even started to stoop until an enlightened teacher had persuaded her to stand up straight, mitigating her height

by simple, well-cut clothes. Deborah had never resigned herself to Leo's chosen style.

Now Leo said tolerantly, 'I dress like this to stay cool and
look reasonably professional during a long working day,
Mother. Besides,' she said as Deborah opened her mouth to
remonstrate, 'I like my clothes.'

Deborah gave her shoulders a little annoyed shake.

'Well, you won't need to look professional tonight. So you
can buy something pretty for once. It's not as if you can't
afford it.'

Leo flung up her hands in a gesture of surrender.

The car delivered them to a small shop. The window was
filled with a large urn holding six-foot grasses. Leo knew the
famous international name. And the prices that went with it.
Her heart sank.

'It's lucky I paid off my credit card bill just last week,
isn't it?' she said.

Deborah ignored this poor spirited remark. 'We're going
to buy you something special,' she said firmly, urging her
reluctant daughter out of the car.

'Here comes the frill patrol,' groaned Leo.

But she did her mother an injustice. Deborah clearly han-
kered after a cocktail suit in flowered brocade. But she gave
in gracefully when Leo said, 'It makes me look like a newly
upholstered sofa.' Instead they came away with georgette
harem pants, the colour of bark, and a soft jacket in a golden
apricot. Deborah gave her a long silk scarf in bronze and
amber to go with it.

'Thank you mother,' said Leo, touched.

Deborah blinked rapidly. 'I wish you were wearing it to
go out to dinner with someone more exciting than me.'

For a shockingly irrational moment, Leo's thoughts flew
to her mystery rescuer. She felt her colour rise. Inwardly she
cursed her revealing porcelain skin and the shadowy Amer
with equal fury. To say nothing of her mother's sharp eyes.

'Ah,' said Deborah. 'Anyone I know?'

'There's no one,' said Leo curtly.

She stamped out to the limousine. Deborah said a more graceful farewell to the sales staff before she followed.

'Darling,' she began as soon as the driver had closed the door on her, 'I think we need to have a little talk.'

Leo stared in disbelief. 'I'm twenty-four, Mother. I know about the birds and the bees.'

Deborah pursed her lips. 'I'm glad to hear it. Not that anyone would think it from the way you go on.'

'Mother—' said Leo warningly.

'It's all right. I don't want to know about your boy-friends. I want to talk about marriage.'

Leo blinked. 'You're getting married again?'

Deborah enjoyed the attentions of a number of escorts but she had never shown any sign of wanting to have her pretty Holland Park house invaded by a male in residence.

Now Deborah clicked her tongue in irritation. 'Of course not. I mean *your* marriage.'

Leo was blank. 'But I'm not getting married.'

'Ah,' said Deborah again. She started to play with an earring. 'Then the rumours about you and Simon Hartley aren't true?'

Leo stared at her in genuine bewilderment. 'Simon Hartley? Dad's new Chief Accountant? I hardly know him.'

Deborah twiddled the earring harder. 'I thought he was the brother of a school friend of yours.'

Leo made a surprised face. 'Claire Hartley, yes. But he's quite a bit older than us.'

'So you've never met him?'

Leo shrugged. 'Dad brought him out here a couple of months ago. Some sort of familiarisation trip. All the Adventures in Time staff met him.'

'And did you like him?'

Leo gave a snort of exasperation. 'Come off it, Mother. The strain is showing. Believe me, there's no point in trying to make matches for me. I'm not like you. I honestly don't think I'm cut out for marriage.'

Slightly to her surprise, Deborah did not take issue with

that. Instead she looked thoughtful. 'Why not? Because you've got too much to do being Gordon Groom's heir?'

Leo tensed. Here it comes, she thought. This is where she starts to attack Pops.

She said stiffly, 'I chose to go into the company.'

Deborah did not take issue with that, either. She said abruptly, 'Leo, have you ever been in love?'

Leo could not have been more taken aback if her mother had asked her if she had ever flown to the moon.

'Excuse me?'

The moment she said it, she could have kicked herself. Deborah would take her astonishment as an admission of failure with the opposite sex. Just what she had always warned her daughter would happen if she did not lighten up, in fact.

'I thought not.'

But Deborah did not sound triumphant. She sounded worried. And for what must have been the first time in her life she did not push the subject any further.

It made Leo feel oddly uneasy. She was used to maternal lectures. She could deal with them. A silent, preoccupied Deborah was something new in her experience. She did not like it.

Amer had given Hari a number of instructions which had caused his friend's eyebrows to climb higher and higher. He took dutiful notes, however. But at the final instruction he put down his monogrammed pen and looked at Amer with burning reproach.

'What am I going to tell your father?'

'Don't tell him anything,' said Amer fluently. 'You report back to my uncle the Minister of Health. My uncle will tell him that I made the speech I was sent here to make. *Et voilà.*'

'But they will expect you to say something at the dinner.'

Amer gave him a wry smile. 'You say it. You wrote it, after all. You'll be more convincing than I will.'

Hari bit back an answering smile. 'They'll find out,' he said gloomily. 'What will they say?'

'I don't care what a bunch of dentists say,' Amer told him with breezy arrogance.

'I wasn't thinking of the dentists,' Hari said ironically, 'I was thinking of your uncle the Health Minister, your uncle the Finance Minister, your uncle the Oil Minister...'

Amer's laugh had a harsh ring. 'I don't care what they think, either.'

'But your father—'

'If my father isn't very careful,' Amer said edgily, 'I shall go back to university and turn myself into the archaeologist I was always meant to be.'

Hari was alarmed. 'It's my fault, isn't it? I shouldn't have said that the women you know were programmed to think you are wonderful. You've taken it as a challenge, haven't you?'

Amer chuckled. 'Let us say you outlined a hypothesis which I would be interested to test.'

'But why Miss Roberts?'

Amer hesitated for the briefest moment. Then he gave a small shrug. 'Why not?'

'You said she was like stale bread,' Hari reminded him.

Amer's well-marked brows twitched together in a frown. 'I hope you weren't thinking of telling her that,' he warned.

'I'm not telling her anything,' said Hari hastily. 'I'm not going anywhere near her.'

Amer frowned even more blackly. 'Don't be ridiculous. That's not the way to stop me seeing her.'

'I'm not being ridiculous,' said Hari. A thought occurred to him. He was beginning to enjoy himself. 'If you want to play at being an ordinary guy, the first thing you'll have to do is fix up a date in person like the rest of us.'

There was a startled pause. Then Amer began to laugh softly.

'But of course. I never intended anything else. That's part of the fun.'

'Fun!'

'Of course. New experiments are always fun.'

'So she's a new experiment. Are you going to tell her that?' Hari asked politely.

'I don't know what I'm going to tell her yet,' Amer said with disarming frankness. 'I suppose it partly depends on what she tells me.' He looked intrigued at the thought.

'The first thing she'll tell you is your name, title and annual income,' snapped Hari, goaded.

But Amer was not to be shaken out of his good humour.

'I've been thinking about that. If she hasn't recognised me so far, she isn't going to unless someone tells her. So you'd better make the arrangements in your name.'

'Oh? And what about when you turn up instead of me? Even if you can convince the maître d' to be discreet what about the other people at the restaurant?'

'I've thought of that, too.' Amer was as complacent as a cat. 'Now here's what I want you to do—'

Back at the hotel Leo found her father had tried to return her call twice. He had left a series of numbers where he could be contacted. Immediately, according to the message. So he was serious about it.

Leo tapped the message against her teeth. She did not look forward to it. But years of dealing with her father had taught her that it was better to face up to his displeasure sooner rather than later. She squared her shoulders and dialled.

'What's happened?' Gordon Groom said, cutting through her enquiries after his health and well-being.

Leo sighed and told him.

She kept it short. Her father liked his reports succinct. He had been known to fire an executive for going on longer than Gordon wanted.

When she finished, slightly to her surprise, his first thought was for Mrs Silverstein. 'How is she?'

'Sleeping, I think.'

'Check on her,' Gordon ordered. 'And again before you go to bed.'

'Of course,' said Leo, touched.

'There's a real up side opportunity here. The retired American market has a lot of growth potential for us,' Gordon went on, oblivious.

That was more like the father Leo knew. She suppressed a grin. 'I'll check.'

'And what about Ormerod? Has he lost it?'

Leo shifted uncomfortably. She had been very firm with her father that she was not going to Cairo to spy on the existing management.

'Some of the local customer care is a bit archaic,' she said carefully.

'Sounds like they need an operational audit.' Gordon dismissed the Cairo office from his mind and turned his attention to his daughter. 'Now what about you? Not much point in making Ormerod take you back, is there?'

Leo shuddered. 'No.'

Her father took one of his lightning executive decisions. 'Then you'd better come back to London. Our sponsorship program needs an overhaul. You can do that until—' He stopped. 'You can take charge of that.'

Leo was intrigued. But she knew her father too well to press him. The last thing he was going to do was tell her the job he had in mind for her until he had made sure that she was up to it.

'Okay. I'll clear up things here and come home.'

Other fathers, Leo thought, would have been glad. Other fathers would have said, 'It'll be great to have you home, darling.' Or even, 'Let me know the flight, I'll come to the airport and meet you.'

Gordon just said, 'You've still got your keys?'

They shared a large house in Wimbledon. But Leo had her own self-contained flat. She and her father did not interfere with each other.

'I've still got my keys,' she agreed.

'See you when you get back.' Clearly about to ring off, a thought struck Gordon. 'You haven't heard from your mother, by the way?'

'As a matter of fact she's here. I'm having dinner with her tonight.'

Gordon did not bad mouth Deborah the way she did him but you could tell that he was not enthusiastic about the news, Leo thought.

'Oh? Well, don't let her fill your head with any of her silly ideas,' he advised. 'See you.'

He rang off.

Leo told herself she was not hurt. He was a good and conscientious father. But he had no truck with sentimentality; especially not if it showed signs of interfering with business.

It was silly to think that she would have liked him to be a bit more indignant on her behalf, Leo thought. When Deborah had ranted about Roy Ormerod, Leo had calmed her down. Yet when her father didn't, she felt unloved.

'The trouble with me is, I don't know what I want,' Leo told herself. 'Forget it.'

But she could not help remembering how the dark-eyed stranger had stood up to Ormerod for her. It had made her feel—what? Protected? Cared for? She grimaced at the thought.

'No regression to frills,' she warned herself. 'You're a Groom executive. You can't afford to turn to mush.'

Anyway she would not see the mysterious stranger again. Just as well if he had this sort of effect on her usual robust independence.

She made a dinner reservation for herself and her mother. Then she stripped off the day's dusty clothes and ran a bath. The hotel provided everything you needed, she saw wryly, even a toothbrush and a luxurious monogrammed bathrobe.

She sank into scented foam and let her mind go into free fall. When the phone rang on the bathroom wall, she ignored it, lifting a long foot to turn on the tap and top up the warm water. For the first time in months, it seemed, she did not have to worry about a tour or a function or timetable inconsistencies. She tipped her head back and gave herself up to the pleasures of irresponsibility.

There was a knock at the door.

Mother come to make sure I've plucked my eyebrows, diagnosed Leo. She won't go away. Oh well, time to get going, I suppose.

She raised the plug and got out of the bath. She knotted the bathrobe round her and opened the door, trying to assume a welcoming expression. When she saw who it was, she stopped trying in pure astonishment.

'You! What do you want?'

'Very welcoming,' said the mysterious stranger, amused. 'How about a date?'

'A *date?*'

'Dinner,' he explained fluently. 'Music, dancing, cultural conversation. Whatever you feel like.'

Leo shook her head to clear it.

'But—a date? With me?'

A faint hint of annoyance crossed the handsome face. 'Why not?'

Because men don't ask me on dates. Not out of the blue. Not without an introduction and several low-key meetings at the houses of mutual friends. Not without knowing who my father is.

Leo crushed the unworthy thought.

'When?' she said, playing for time while she got her head round this new experience.

'Tonight or never,' he said firmly.

'Oh well, that settles it.' Leo was not sure whether she was disappointed or relieved. But at least the decision was taken for her. 'I'm already going out to dinner tonight.'

She made to close the door. It did not work.

He did not exactly put his foot in the door, but he leaned against the doorjamb as if he was prepared to stay there all night.

'Cancel.' His tone said it was a suggestion rather than an order. His eyes said it was a challenge.

Leo found herself reknotting the sash of her borrowed robe in an agitated manner and saying, 'No,' in a voice like the primmest teacher she had ever had at her polite girls' school.

He bit back a smile. 'I dare you.'

She looked at him with dislike. 'I suppose you think that makes it irresistible?'

'Well, interesting, anyway.'

If Leo was honest, his smile was more than intriguing. She felt her heart give an odd little jump, as if it had been pushed out of a nice, safe burrow and wanted to climb back in again. She knew that feeling. She hated taking chances and always had.

She looked at the man and thought: I don't know where going out with this man would take me. Thank God I'm spending the evening with Mother.

And then, as if some particularly mischievous gods were listening, along the corridor came Deborah Groom. Leo groaned.

'Is that a yes, no or maybe?' said Amer, entertained.

'None of the above. Hello, Mother.'

He turned quickly. Deborah did not hesitate. Assuming that the man at Leo's door was Roy Ormerod, she stormed straight into battle.

'How dare you come here and harass my daughter? Haven't you done enough? I shall make sure your employer knows all about this.'

Amer blinked. A look of unholy appreciation came into his eyes.

'I didn't mean to harass her,' he said meekly.

Leo writhed inwardly. 'Mother, please. This is Mr—' thankfully she remembered his name just in time '—Mr Amer. He was the one who persuaded the hotel to find me a room.'

'Oh.'

Deborah took a moment to assimilate the information.

Then another to assess Amer. The quality of his tailoring was not lost on her, any more than it had been on her daughter.

'Oh,' she said again in quite a different voice. She held out a gracious hand. 'How kind of you, Mr Amer. I'm Deborah, er, Roberts, Leo's mother.'

'Leo?' he murmured, bowing over her hand.

'Ridiculous, isn't it? Especially with a pretty name like Leonora. After my grandmother, you know. But her father always called her Leo. And it just stuck.'

'Mother,' protested Leo.

Neither of them paid any attention to her.

'Leonora,' he said as if he were savouring it.

Deborah beamed at him. 'And how kind of you to check on Leo.'

He was rueful. 'I was hoping to persuade her to have dinner with me. But she is already engaged.' He sighed but the dark grey eyes were sharp.

Deborah put her pretty head on one side.

'Well, now, isn't that odd? I was just coming to tell Leo that I really didn't feel like going out this evening.' She allowed her shoulders to droop theatrically. 'This heat is so tiring.'

Leo could not believe this treachery.

'What heat, Mother? Every single place you've been today is air conditioned within an inch of its life.'

Deborah looked annoyed. Amer's lips twitched. But, strategist that he was, he did not say anything.

Deborah recovered fast. 'Well, that's exactly the problem.' She turned to Amer appealingly. 'We English aren't used to real air-conditioning. I think I must have caught a chill.' She managed a ladylike cough.

Leo felt murderous. She was almost sure the beastly man was laughing at both of them.

'Then you'd better stay in your room,' she said firmly. 'We'll order room service.'

Deborah gave her a faint, brave smile. 'Oh no, darling. I'll be better on my own. You go and enjoy yourself with Mr Amer.'

Amer took charge before Leo could scream with fury or announce that the last thing in the world she would enjoy was an evening with him.

'If you are sure, Mrs Roberts?' he said smoothly, as if that was all it took to decide the matter. He nodded to Leo, careful not to let his satisfaction show. 'Then I shall look forward to our excursion, Miss Roberts. Shall we say, half an hour?'

He walked off down the corridor before Leo could respond.

'*Mother,*' she said between her teeth.

Deborah was unrepentant. 'Just what you need,' she said briskly, ceasing to droop. 'An evening with a seriously sexy article like that. Should have happened years ago. Now what are you going to wear?'

Leo knew when she was beaten. She stood aside to let her mother come in.

'There's not a lot of choice,' she said drily. 'My work suit. Or the sun flower job you've just talked me into.'

Deborah flung open the wardrobe door and considered the ensemble with a professional eye. 'That will do. It's versatile enough. How smart do you think it will be?'

Leo sighed in exasperation. 'I haven't the slightest idea. I only met the man once before you thrust me into this evening's fiasco.'

If she thought that the information would make Deborah apologise, she mistook her mother. Deborah was intrigued.

'Determined, isn't he? Very flattering.'

'Oh please,' said Leo in disgust.

Deborah ignored that. 'We should have bought you some shoes,' she said in a dissatisfied voice.

Leo picked up her low-heeled black pumps and held them to her protectively. 'They're comfortable.'

Deborah sighed. 'Oh well, they'll have to do. At least, there's stuff in the bathroom to polish them up a bit. Now what about make-up?'

Leo gave up. In her element, Deborah took charge. She shook her head over the ragged ends of Leo's newly washed hair and took her nails scissors to it. After that, she gave her a brief but professional make-up which emphasised Leo's long silky lashes and made her eyes look enormous. She ended by pressing onto her a magnificent pair of topaz drop earrings.

'I'm not used to all this,' protested Leo, surrendering her neat pearl studs with misgiving. 'I'm going to make a terrible fool of myself.'

'You'll be fine,' said Deborah.

But she did not pretend to misunderstand Leo's doubts.

'Darling, you're so capable. You can handle anything, not like me. How have you got this hang up about men?'

'It's not a hang up,' said Leo drily. 'It's the sure and certain knowledge that any man who goes out with me has been turned down by everyone else in the netball team. Unless he thinks he's dating my father.'

Deborah shook her head. 'I don't understand you.'

'I do,' muttered Leo.

'So explain it to me.'

'Big feet and too much bosom,' said Leo baldly. 'Plus a tendency to break things.'

Deborah was shocked. 'Leo! You have a wonderful figure. Think of all those girls out there having to buy padded bras. Men just love curves like yours.'

'Oh sure. A demolition expert with feet like flippers is pretty irresistible, too.'

Deborah sighed but she was a realist. 'Look, darling, men can be very unkind but they're not difficult to deal with if you know how. Tonight, just listen to the man as if he's an oracle. And try not to bump into the furniture.'

Leo's laugh was hollow.

CHAPTER THREE

THERE was no furniture to bump into.

First, Amer arrived in designer jeans and a loose jacket that was the last word in careless chic and made Leo feel seriously overdressed. Then, he announced that they were going out of Cairo. To Leo's increasing trepidation, this involved a short trip in a private helicopter.

'Where are we?' she said, when the helicopter set down and its ailerons stopped turning.

The airstrip was abnormally deserted. In her experience Egyptian airports heaved like anthills.

But her horribly hip companion just smiled.

The briefest ride in an open Jeep took them to a dark landing stage. The stars, like a watchmaker's store of diamond chips, blinked at the water. Silent as a snake, the river gleamed back. There was a warm breeze off the water, like the breath of a huge, sleepy animal.

Leo was not cold; but she shivered.

'Where *are* we?'

'Seventy miles up river from Cairo,' Amer told her coolly.

'Seventy—' Leo broke off, in shock. 'Why?'

'I wanted to give you a picnic by moonlight,' Amer said in soulful tones. He added, more practically, 'You can't do proper moonlight in the middle of a city.'

Leo looked at him in the deepest suspicion. Standing as they were in the headlights of the Jeep it was difficult to tell but she was almost certain he was laughing at her.

The dark harem pants wafted in the breeze. Her gold jacket felt garish under the stars and ridiculously out of place. She felt as clumsily conspicuous as she used to do at agonizing teenage parties.

'Why would you want to take me on a moonlit picnic?' she muttered resentfully. 'You know I thought I was signing up for dinner in a restaurant. Look at me.'

Amer was supervising the removal of a large picnic basket from the jeep. He turned his head at that. He looked her up and down. In the jeep's headlights, Leo somehow felt as if she were on display. She huddled the jacket round her in pure instinct.

'Do you want to go back?' he asked.

It should have been a courteous enquiry. It was not. It was a challenge. On the point of demanding just that, Leo stopped, disconcerted.

After a day of shocks, was this one so terrible, after all? At least it promised a new experience. Who knows, she might actually enjoy it. And she did not have to bother about an early night, for once. She did not have to get up in the small hours to meet an incoming flight. She would never have to again.

'I suppose, now we're here…' she said at last.

Amer raised his eyebrows. It was hardly enthusiastic.

'Shall we call it an experiment then? For both of us.' He sounded rueful.

The driver took the picnic basket down the slope to a wooden jetty. Amer held out a hand to help Leo. The bank was steep. He went first.

She took his hand and scrambled down the dusty path unsteadily. His arm felt like rock, as she swayed and stumbled. It also felt electric, as if just by holding on to him, Leo plugged herself in to some powerhouse of energy. She held her breath and did her best to ignore the tingle that his touch sent through her.

Amer seemed unaware of it. Leo did not know whether that was more of a relief or an irritant. How could the man have this effect on her and not know it? But if he did know it what would he do about it?

'Blast,' she said, exasperated.

He looked back at her. 'What was that?'

Hurriedly she disguised it. 'I turned my ankle over.'

She began limping heavily. Amer came back a couple of steps and put a supporting arm round her, hoisting her with her own petard. It felt like fire.

'Thank you,' said Leo between her teeth.

On the jetty Leo stopped dead.

'It's a dhow,' she exclaimed, half delighted, half alarmed.

The little boat did not look stable. She swayed gently against her mooring rope. There was an oil lamp on the prow; no other light but the stars.

Leo edged forward gingerly. And mother warned me not to bump into the furniture, she thought. With my luck I could have the whole boat over.

A sailor greeted them politely before taking the picnic basket on board. Amer turned and gave a few crisp instructions in Arabic to the driver.

Leo peered at the dark interior of the boat. She thought she could see cushions. They seemed a long way down.

The driver vaulted into the Jeep and gunned the engine. Amer turned back and took in Leo's wariness.

'Are you going to tell me you're seasick?' he said, amused.

Leo cast him an harassed look. Nothing was going to serve her but the truth, she realised.

'I am not the best co-ordinated person in the world,' she announced defiantly. 'I was just trying to work out how to get into this thing.'

The jeep roared off. It left behind the starlit dark and the soft slap of the river against the jetty. And the man, now no more than a dark shadow against shadows. It was a warm night. But in the sudden quiet, Leo shivered.

'That's easy,' Amer said softly.

He picked her up.

'Careful,' gasped Leo, clutching him round the neck.

She could feel the ripple of private laughter under her hands. Amer held her high against his chest and stepped down into the boat.

She was right. There were cushions everywhere. Amer

sank gracefully into them. He seemed, thought Leo, to hold
on to her for far longer that was necessary. She inhaled the
new aroma of expensive laundry and man's skin, all mixed
with some elusive cologne that was hardly there and yet
which she knew she would never forget.

None of the semidetached men in her life had made her
feel like this. Was it because he was, as her mother had called
him, a seriously sexy article? Would any woman have felt
her pulses race in this situation? Or was it only Leo? Had
her cool temperament and shaky experience led her to over-
react to an embrace that was not an embrace at all?
Somewhere deep inside there was still a clumsy sixteen-year-
old who had hung around at the edge of the room at parties,
marooned in her own self-consciousness. Had someone found
the route to reach her at last?

If so, Leo was far from grateful. She disentangled herself,
not without difficulty, and sat up. She pulled her jacket
straight and smoothed her hair.

'Thank you,' she said primly.

'My pleasure.'

She believed him. There was a note in his voice that said
he was enjoying himself hugely. Leo was suddenly grateful
to the darkness. It meant he could not see the colour in her
hot cheeks.

She moved along the cushioned seat to leave a small but
definite space between them. Amer glanced down, noting it.
But he did not object. Instead he called out to the boatman
and they pushed off from the side.

The light breeze took them quickly out to midstream.
Amer leaned back among his cushions and looked at the
stars.

'How is your astronomy?'

'Not very good.'

'Mine is excellent. Let me be your guide.'

Leo looked up reluctantly. It hurt her neck but she was
determined not to lounge at her ease as he was doing. She

was not going to pretend she felt comfortable when she did not.

Amer began to point out the stars by name. He knew a lot of them. The strain on her neck became intolerable. Almost without realising she was doing it, she eased the pain by sliding down until she, too, was reclining among the cushions. Out of the darkness she thought she caught a gleam of white teeth as he smiled. But he was too clever to offer any comment. Far less to touch her.

Oh boy, am I out of my depth here, thought Leo.

The lamp at the prow swung with the motion of the boat, sending waves of shadow over them as if they were under the river instead of on it. She could hear the soft lapping of the water and the unhurried rhythm of his breathing. Nothing else.

Leo did not take her eyes off the stars. But she knew that Amer was less than a hand's length away from her. She had only to turn her body a fraction and they would be touching. She thought: I have never felt so totally alone with anyone in my whole life.

She became aware of the sound of her own breathing. She shivered a little.

'You are cold,' said Amer, coming to halt in mid-discourse on the starscape.

He sat up and shrugged out of his jacket. Leo turned her head. At that angle she had to look up at him. She caught her breath. For a moment it was as if they lay in a bed, drowsing among habitually shared pillows.

At the thought, her whole body convulsed. She jackknifed upright so violently that the frail craft dipped.

The boatman turned his head with a surprised question. Amer answered him, laughing.

He slid the jacket round her shoulders.

'How jumpy you are.' It sounded like a caress.

To Leo, shaking badly now with reaction, it felt as if he had reached out and run his hand over her flesh, though not an inch of skin was exposed. She huddled his jacket round her. Then realised that it still held the warmth of his body and wished she hadn't.

She swallowed. Loudly.

He did not move any closer. But he reached out a lazy hand and brushed her hair outside his jacket's collar. Leo went very still. It felt as if he owned her.

'Your hair is like silk,' Amer murmured. 'But too short.'

Leo had an involuntary picture of the two of them lying in bed, Amer propped on one elbow, running his free hand through her yards of soft and shining hair. It was so vivid that she almost believed he could see it as well. Her whole body buzzed with shock and embarrassment.

'It used to be long,' she said, her voice too high and fast. 'All through school. I used to be able to sit on it. But when I got older and tried to pin it up, it was too fine. So it was always collapsing. And then my boy friend in college said he couldn't sleep with it, because it was always getting wound round him or getting in his mouth…' She wished she hadn't said that. She was gabbling and she knew it.

Amer held up a hand to stop the flow.

'Don't tell me about other men,' he said in a pained voice.

Leo gasped. The light on the prow swung as the boat tacked. It showed him lounging among the cushions, regarding her quizzically.

'You really don't know how to play this game, do you?'

'What game?' said Leo.

Though she knew. Her racing pulse had been telling her ever since he picked her up and put her in the boat. Now she was almost sure he was smiling in the darkness.

'That's an interesting question,' he said thoughtfully. 'Maybe somewhere between a contest and a carnival. What do you think?'

Leo swallowed. He was right. This was a completely new game for her. She had no idea how to riposte.

'I think I'm in over my head,' she said honestly.

There was a pause as if she had surprised him. Not entirely pleasantly.

Then, 'Hey. You're supposed to be enjoying yourself, you know.'

Amer moved. At once her muscles clenched. She was burningly conscious of his body. He was so close, she could sense the latent power of him. And it was not fear that kept her alert and trembling, she realised.

But he was only stretching, making himself more comfortable. He put his arms behind his head and looked up at her thoughtfully. As the light swung again, she saw that he had pushed up the sleeves of his shirt. The brief glimpse of muscular forearms did unwelcome things to her stomach.

The boat tacked again and the light swung in the other direction. Leo tried to gasp for air quietly. She had not realised she was holding her breath.

She cleared her throat. 'Where are we going? I mean, is this it?'

Amer gave a soft laugh.

'Hungry are you?'

Leo decided to assume he was talking about food.

'Well breakfast was at five o clock this morning and I haven't eaten since,' she told him.

'Good grief.' He sounded genuinely horrified. 'We must do something about that at once.'

He said something in quick Arabic to the boatman. The boat turned.

'What happened?' Amer demanded. 'The revenge of the unreasonable boss?'

Leo shook her head, laughing. 'Nope. That's normal at this time of year.'

'It sounds like slavery. Why do you do it?'

Leo felt better now they were discussing an ordinary subject at last. She could do polite conversation, she thought ruefully. It was subtle sexual repartee that defeated her.

'It's my job,' she said.

'Why did you choose a job like that?'

Leo thought about her father's announcement of her two-year assignment.

'Well, the job sort of found me,' she said ruefully. 'My chief told me where I was going. I didn't get a vote.'

'Then you should have looked for a new job with a more modern chief.' He sounded impatient.

Leo bridled at his tone.

'It's easy to say that if you have an infinite range of choices open to you. Most of us don't.'

Amer gave a bark of laughter. 'No one has infinite choice. Most people have fewer than you think.'

'Are you telling me that you're a slave of circumstance, too?' Leo challenged him mockingly.

He did not like that. He said curtly, 'We are not talking about me.'

And that, she thought, sounded like an order.

The boat was skirting a small island. It came to rest against the bank. The boatman moored it fore and aft and lowered the sail. He unhooked the lamp from the prow and brought it down to them.

Amer motioned to him to set out the picnic basket. Then waved him away. The man leaped over the side of the boat and disappeared into the darkness. All Leo's returning confidence went with him.

She thought Amer would expect her to unpack the basket and serve the food. But he did not. Instead he filled warm ovals of pitta bread with a deliciously aromatic salad and gave one to her. Watching his deft movements, Leo thought: He thinks if he left it to me, I'd drop the food all over the cushions. The truth was she thought so, too. It added to her constraint.

'Thank you,' she said in a subdued voice.

She sat up, curling her legs under her, away from him.

'Drink?'

There was tea, sherbet, juices. Leo chose water and drank a whole glassful.

Amer raised an amused eyebrow. 'You've got a real desert thirst there.'

'Anxiety always makes me thirsty,' Leo said unwarily.

He grimaced. 'Ouch.'

'What? Oh.' She bit her lip. 'That sounded rude. I didn't mean—'

'I think we both know what you meant,' he said drily.

Now the soft light was at their end of the boat and hardly swaying at all, he would see her blush. Leo cursed her porcelain-pale skin. It was always giving her away.

She said stiffly, 'I'm sorry.'

Amer did not answer for a moment. Leo hesitated; then dared a look at him under her eyelashes. His expression was unreadable.

'You're an education,' he said at last. 'I'm very much afraid that Hari was right.'

Leo was confused. 'Who's Hari?'

He gave an unexpected laugh. 'But then, I was right, too,' he went on unheeding. 'You're nobody's toy, are you? You're your own person. Right through to the beautiful frankness.'

Leo knew she was being mocked and did not like it. 'I've said I'm sorry,' she muttered.

'Don't be sorry.' He was amused again. 'You should be proud to be a truth teller. There aren't so many of them around.'

Leo wished she had her glasses to hide behind. In their absence, she munched on the pitta.

It was odd. She should have been starving after the turbulent day. But the last thing she wanted was food. If Amer would only stop looking at her like that, as if he had never seen anything like her, she would have turned away from the food with relief.

But Amer continued to play the attentive host, offering her delicacies from the basket and keeping up a steady flow of informative conversation. The Nile, the desert sky, ancient temples, modern dams—he covered them all while Leo worked her way stolidly through more calories than she cared to count. Eventually he gave her a thimbleful of thin, sharp coffee and said, 'Your turn.'

It was the moment Leo had been dreading. 'My, er, turn?'

'Talk to me,' he commanded.

'What—' Her voice wavered. She took command of it and started again. 'What shall I talk about?'

He gave a soft laugh. 'It is usual to start with whatever you want the other party to know about you.'

'But I *don't* want you to know anything about me,' Leo said unguardedly. There was more truth in that than she would have been willing to admit, if she had thought about it.

Amer took it calmly. 'Then tell me what I want to know.'

'Like what?' said Leo warily.

'Like where you come from. How you ended up in Cairo. How the men in your life like it.'

Leo considered. Nothing too private there, she thought.

So she said readily enough, 'I come from London—well a suburb of London. My company is basically an international hotel chain. They diversified into other leisure areas, including this local travel agency, and sent me out here for two years. To get experience of work at the coal face, so to speak. I've been here just over a year. Eventually I'll go back to Head Office.' She sighed. 'After the row with Roy sooner rather than later.'

'And the men in your life?' he prompted.

'Ah.'

Well, it was not *private*, exactly but Leo was not sure she wanted to discuss her romantic failures with this unreadable man. On the other hand, her father had taught her that the truth was never damaging. And after tonight she would never see Mr Amer again.

She squared her shoulders and said cheerfully, 'No men.'

His eyes narrowed. She caught the flicker of long lashes against the dark.

'Not even—what did you call him?—Roy?' he asked. He did not sound very interested. His tone was almost idle.

She gave a snort of laughter at the thought.

Amer did not share her amusement. 'So how did he manage to throw you out of your flat?' he demanded, swift as a striking snake.

It shocked her into silence.

'I asked you if you lived with him, if you remember. You did not answer then, either.'

Leo had the sudden impression of fierce anger. She searched the shadowed face. He did not say any more but his silence was somehow relentless.

She said hurriedly, 'It was a company flat.'

Still he did not say anything.

Leo found her tone was placating, as if he had accused her of something. 'We go out of Cairo so much with the tourist parties that it's not worth having a flat each. We all share. Roy, Vanessa, Kevin, anyone else that comes out. Truly. Roy wasn't there most of the time.'

Amer digested this for a moment. 'Not much privacy then,' he said at last.

To Leo's relief it seemed as if he was no longer angry. Instead he sounded thoughtful. 'Is that the reason?'

'Reason?' Leo echoed, puzzled.

She caught the flash of white as he smiled. 'You said there were no men in your life,' he reminded her.

'Oh that!'

She was oddly relieved that he had decided to believe her. What could it matter whether a stranger trusted her word, after all? She would never see him again after tonight. But she was glad and she knew it.

'Yes *that*,' he mimicked her, teasing. 'If there are no men in your life there has to be a reason.'

And he was going to persist until she told him. Leo sighed and gave him the truth.

'I don't really *work* with men, if you know what I mean. Never have. Not really. Drives my mother mad.'

She felt him considering it. She gave him a quick, bright smile. But she could not sustain it. Her eyes slid away from him before she could read his expression.

He said thoughtfully, 'Does that mean you are not attracted to men?'

Leo was startled. 'Oh *no*. Well, at least, I haven't thought about it much. I've had a couple of sort of relationships. Pretty low-grade stuff. The guys walked away after a bit and to be honest it was a relief. I don't think I'm designed to stroke the male ego. Well not for long.'

Amer stiffened. 'There is more to a relationship between a man and a woman than ego stroking.'

'Is there?' Leo said drily. 'Didn't seem that way to me.'

This time she managed to look at him for longer. There was no doubt she had annoyed him. He was still smiling but his displeasure was tangible.

Leo was surprised; and then amused. Amer must have thought she would turn to toffee under his stylish not-quite-seduction. It was pleasant to have knocked his assumptions off course, however slightly.

He said shortly, 'It sounds as if you have been unfortunate in your encounters.'

Leo shrugged. 'No, I'd say it was pretty standard.'

'On the basis of—what did you call them?—a couple of low-grade relationships?'

She looked at him ironically. 'I don't just know about my own mistakes. Girls talk you know.'

'In that case,' Amer said triumphantly, 'you must know that most girls these days would have more than a couple of unsatisfactory experiments to base their theories on.'

'Ah but most girls keep on trying. They've got to. They want to marry.'

Amer was taken aback.

'And you don't?'

Leo shifted her shoulders. In her head she could hear Deborah saying anxiously, 'Darling, how on earth do you think you're going to get married if you go on like this?' She managed not to wince.

'I'd say the odds are against it,' she said evenly.

Amer noticed the evasion. 'You mean you *do* want to but

you don't think it's going to happen.' He sounded a lot more content with that.

It made Leo furious. She sat bolt upright, rocking the small craft again with the violence of the movement.

'Look,' she said, 'I said I'd have dinner with you. I didn't agree to be dissected because you happen to have a nasty taste in dinner party conversation.'

'Is that what I've been doing?' He sounded startled and not very pleased.

There was a pause while he considered it. Then he said in amusement, 'All right. Take your revenge. I'll tell you anything you want to know.'

'No, thank you,' said Leo distantly. 'I don't want to dissect you, either.'

He shook his head, still deeply amused. 'Still telling the truth? Not great tactics—but very impressive.'

'Thank you,' said Leo, not meaning it.

He stretched. The fine cotton stretched, too, across taut muscles. Leo remembered how those muscles had felt under her fingers when he put her into the boat and her mouth was suddenly dry.

'Look at that moon,' Amer said, unheeding. He sounded as self-congratulatory as if he had arranged it personally, Leo thought.

She looked up. The moon was not quite full, a champagne sorbet among all the diamond chips. She thought she had never seen it so clear or the sky so close. It made her feel slightly dazed. She closed her eyes against the whirling sensation.

Amer said softly, 'Puts human nonsense in perspective, doesn't it?'

Leo opened her mouth to demand whether her views fell into the category of human nonsense. Only then she opened her eyes. And found herself looking straight into his. The whirling sensation increased.

Hardly knowing what she did, she subsided among the cushions. She could not take her eyes off him.

Amer did not touch her. He did not even lean over her, though his eyes scanned her face intently.

'Yes,' he said, as if he was answering something she said.

Leo thought: I want him. He knows I want him. I've never felt like this before in my life. I didn't know I could feel like this.

He lowered himself until he was leaning on his elbow among the cushions, looking down at her. Leo felt as if he could see straight through her. He saw the defences; went through them to her galloping confusion; smiled, and went through that, too, right into her soul.

She went very still. They were as close as lovers. But still he did not touch.

She had thought she was immune. It was other girls who waited sleepless by the phone. Other girls who held their breath when their man looked at them.

Leo thought: their man? *Their* man? I am laying claim to this man, now? When he hasn't even kissed me? I don't even want him to kiss me. Do I?

The boatman was coming back. She heard his friendly greeting. Felt the small movement in the boat as he came aboard.

Amer did not move. Nor did Leo. She could feel her eyes widening, widening...

The boatman was busying himself with the sail.

Amer said softly, 'Shall I tell him to go away again and leave us alone for a couple of hours?'

The studded sky wheeled behind his head.

'I don't know what you mean.' Leo spoke with difficulty.

He was so close she could feel his little puffed breath of frustration. She thought: Why doesn't he touch me? But still he did not.

Instead he murmured, 'That's the first lie you've ever told me.'

She felt a sort of agony at his words.

She thought: No matter what happens now, I'm never going to be the same after this.

She held her breath. But Amer rolled aside and sat up. He gave the boatman a few orders and did not sound annoyed. He did not sound as if he cared very much at all.

Leo let out her breath very carefully. The men talked rapidly. Then the boatman packed the debris of their meal back into the picnic basket. Leo swung her legs aside and sat up, setting the boat rocking wildly. Probably for the first time in her life, she did not apologise. She was too wound up.

She smoothed her hair with a shaking hand. Every tiny area of exposed skin at neck and wrists quivered where the soft breeze brushed against it. She had never been so intensely aware of sensation before; nor of her own sensuality. Never realised so totally that she was a physical creature. Never *wanted*...

Leo halted her thoughts abruptly at that point. Never wanted what? she asked herself fiercely. Amer? Nonsense. Crazy nonsense.

She straightened, folding her hands in her lap. She did not care if she looked prim. She did not care what Amer thought of her at all. She suddenly, desperately, wanted to get back to her room and take stock of what had happened to her.

At least she had not reached for him, Leo thought. She thanked Heaven for that.

Leo was monosyllabic on the return journey. Amer did not push her. He was very much at his ease, courteous but slightly distant. When they entered the hotel he thanked her formally for her company and wished her good-night.

Leo shook hands. 'Thank you,' she said as politely as if he were one of Adventures in Time's regular bus drivers.

Her tone clearly amused him.

'We will meet soon,' he assured her.

Leo had not told him that she was expecting to fly out imminently. She did not tell him now. She just gave him a meaningless smile and headed for the lifts.

Hari knew that the evening had not been a success the moment that Amer walked into the suite. One look at the

Sheikh's face and Hari decided to keep the conversation strictly professional.

'Report of various conversations I had before the dinner,' he said, handing over a slim folder. 'Extract of speeches.' That was a substantial ring binder. 'Oh and a message from His Majesty.' An envelope from the hotel's fax bureau.

'My father can wait,' said Amer, showing his teeth.

Hari did not comment, though he knew what the old Sheikh's views would be if anyone reported that back to him.

'The South of France,' Hari said, consulting his notes. 'I've booked flights for Paris on Thursday. I thought you'd want to stop over.'

Amer was frowning. 'Hold on that for the moment,' he said curtly.

'You want to stay for the reception at the end of the conference?' asked Hari, surprised.

Amer shrugged. 'Maybe.' He paused, his frown dissolving into a speculative look. 'I've got unfinished business in Cairo.'

Hari hid a smile. 'Didn't she like the picnic?' he asked innocently.

'She—' Amer bit it off. 'She is not entirely what I expected. Nor was the evening, for that matter.'

Hari chuckled. 'That's what comes of not telling her who you are.'

Amer shook his head slowly. 'I don't think so. She is unusual. I don't think that would have made any difference at all.'

'In that case, she's not unusual, she's unique,' said the cynical Hari.

Amer was surprised into a sudden laugh. 'You could be right,' he said. He clapped Hari on the shoulder. 'Intriguing, isn't it?'

Leo was not sure whether it was too late to check on Mrs Silverstein. She compromised by knocking very softly on the lady's door. There was no answer.

Oh well, thought Leo, she was probably asleep. She was turning away when one of the hotel staff came running out of the service door. The lady had called room service asking for ice, he said. Then when they tried to deliver it, she had not opened the door.

'When was this?' said Leo with foreboding.

Just ten minutes ago. They had knocked several times.

'Have you got a pass key?'

He nodded.

'Then let's go and see what's happened.'

He was clearly relieved at this decision. He opened the door for Leo.

Mrs Silverstein was lying on the carpet in the main body of the room. Her fall had overturned the coffee table and sent Arabic sweetmeats flying. Her forehead was clammy and she had the beginnings of an almighty bruise on her cheek. But, Leo established, she was breathing.

She summoned a doctor, warning him that the patient would need to be admitted to a clinic fast. He arrived with an ambulance and paramedics and put Mrs Silverstein on oxygen immediately. Leo went with the stretcher.

In the lobby light, Mrs Silverstein opened her eyes. She looked anxious. Leo took her hand.

'It's all right,' she said reassuringly. 'I'm here.'

The weak eyes blinked and focused.

'Looking good,' said Mrs Silverstein, rallying a bit. 'Hot date?'

Leo smiled down at her. 'I've been out to dinner,' she tempered.

'Anyone I know?'

'A guest in the hotel.' Well, it sounded better than pick up, Leo thought ruefully. 'A Mr Amer.'

A beatific smile curved Mrs Silverstein's cherubic lips.

'Sheikh.'

Leo stumbled. 'What?'

'Sheikh Amer el Barbary,' said Mrs Silverstein with satisfaction. 'I looked him up.'

Leo stopped dead and stared. Slow realisation dawned. It was followed by horror.

He had lied to her. Deliberately misled her. Invited her to ask him questions, knowing she wouldn't, when he had already withheld the most important piece of information. Oh what an idiot, he must think her. What an idiot she *was*.

Mrs Silverstein's stretcher was disappearing through the door. Leo broke into a run.

CHAPTER FOUR

SIX months later, Leo could still feel the shock of that realisation. It could bring her awake in the middle of the night, cold with embarrassment. And, at the same time, hot with longing. Which, of course, made the embarrassment worse and did nothing at all for her self-respect.

God knows what she would have said to him, if she had come face-to-face with Amer again. But she did not. Mrs Silverstein needed to be accompanied back to the States. As Leo was leaving Egypt anyway, she jumped at the chance to leave at once.

So now she was in London, trying to restart her life. Without much success.

'What's wrong?' said her friend Claire Hartley, as Leo drove her down to spend the weekend with the Hartley family. 'Missing the pyramids?'

'Not missing one damn thing,' said Leo with rather more emphasis than the casual remark required.

Claire digested this in silence as Leo concentrated on getting through the one way system. Eventually they got onto the motorway and Claire said, 'You've been seeing a lot of brother Simon, haven't you?'

Leo cast her a quick look of surprise. 'Only at work.'

'You went to the Nightingale Ball with him,' Claire reminded her.

Leo grimaced. 'That's work.'

'Then he's got nothing to do with your being glad to be home?'

'I didn't say I was glad to be home,' Leo said patiently. 'I said I didn't miss Cairo. There's a difference.'

'Oh,' said Claire enlightened. 'What happened in Cairo?'

She thought about it. 'Or should I say who happened in Cairo?'

Leo winced. An Arab prince had amused himself for an evening by offering a humble courier a night of high romance and princely luxury. Because that was all it had been for him, an amusement. Leo saw it clearly. That refusal to touch her which had set all her senses aflame and still shot through her dreams, only showed how little he cared whether she responded to him or not.

'That just about covers it,' she said with harsh self-mockery.

Claire had not heard that note in her voice before. 'What happened?'

'One minute I was an independent woman with a small local career problem and no roof over my head. The next— the aliens invaded.'

Claire slewed round on the leather seat and stared at her friend.

'What sort of aliens?'

'Rich, royal and thoroughly irresponsible aliens,' Leo said bitterly. 'Well, one alien.' She ground her teeth, remembering.

Claire was amazed. 'He really hit the spot, didn't he? New experience for you, Mrs Cool.'

Leo's smile was wry. Her reputation for indifference to the opposite sex had started long ago. At her boarding school dances to be precise. Gawky as she was, taller than most of boys and painfully shy, Leo found the best way to deal with being teased was to pretend that she did not care. Neither Claire nor anyone else ever detected the truth. They just thought Leo was too level-headed to suffer the traumas of adolescence. If only they knew!

'Amer el-Barbary would be a new experience for anyone.'

'Sounds like fun,' Claire said enviously. 'Tell.'

Leo looked at the long road ahead of them. In the sun it looked like a stream of melting black toffee. She sighed. It was going to be a long journey.

She told.

Claire was astounded. When Leo finished she sat in stunned silence for a moment. She shook her head in disbelief.

'And you didn't even write to him?'

'What would I have said?' Leo snapped. 'Thank you for an illuminating evening? By the way, I hope this finds you as you didn't bother to give me your real name?'

'There could have been all sorts of reasons for that,' protested Claire.

Leo was more suspicious than her friend. 'Like what?'

'Well, maybe he thought you wouldn't go out with him if you knew he was terribly grand.'

Leo said something very rude. Claire grinned. 'No. All right. Well how about this one—he wanted you to go out with him as a man and not his position in the world.'

Leo snorted. 'I don't believe in fairy stories. He just thought it was amusing to hand me a smooth line. In fact—' for a moment her expression lightened '—he got very annoyed when I didn't respond as predicted.'

'Did he say so?'

'He said we would meet soon,' Leo admitted reluctantly.

Claire made an exasperated noise. 'So you ran away to America with an eighty-year-old widow. Honestly, Leo, I despair of you.' She added curiously, 'Hasn't he tried to get in touch with you?'

'It wouldn't do him any good if he did. All my records have gone from the Cairo office. Nobody there knew who I was. I used my grandmother's name.'

'The office could still forward mail, presumably.'

'I told you,' Leo said patiently, 'they don't know there's anyone to forward it to. None of the staff there know that Miss Roberts is the boss's daughter, Miss Groom.'

Claire shook her head, dissatisfied with this ending to the romance. 'If you saw him again—'

'I'd spit in his eye,' Leo said militantly.

Claire was a good friend but she was not noted for her

tact. 'But it sounds as if you were half-way to falling in love with the guy.'

'Love,' said Leo ferociously, 'is the biggest fairy story of the lot.'

'Most people expect to fall in love at some time or other.' Claire's tone was dry.

Unbidden, Amer's triumphant voice said in her ear, 'You mean you do want to but you don't think it's going to happen.' Admittedly he had been talking about marriage not love. But Leo flushed as violently as if he had been there in the car with them and reading her thoughts.

'Not me,' she said very loudly.

The Trustee of the el-Barbary charitable foundation was having a bad time. Normally Sheikh Amer was more approachable than the old Sheikh. But on this visit he was proving even more difficult than his autocratic father: elusive, preoccupied and now downright irritable. He was tapping his gold fountain pen on his papers as if he could hardly bear to sit through the meeting a minute more.

'Several matters for Sheikh Amer's personal attention.'

Amer did not bother to disguise his impatience. 'Give the list to my assistant.'

The Trustee did not hear. 'Dinner at your college. Oh, I see you've already accepted that. Reception at the Science Museum to launch the second phase of the Antika Research Project. They have asked—'

Amer's face was thunderous. Hari intervened swiftly.

'Shall I deal with those?' he suggested in a soothing voice.

The Trustee handed them over, relieved. But he was a conscientious man.

'Antika have asked if His Excellency will contribute something to their book.'

Amer looked as if he were going to explode.

The Trustee began to gabble. 'Fund-raising. They're bringing out a collection of essays by celebrity sponsors. As His

Excellency is Chairman... They say all the other board members have written something...'

There was a dangerous pause.

Then, 'Get the details,' Amer told Hari curtly. He stood up. 'That concludes the meeting, gentlemen. I have an appointment now, but I hope to join you for lunch later. Hari will show you where to go.'

Hari marshalled them out.

Amer got up and moved restlessly round the room. When a tall, quiet man was shown in, he looked round. His visitor was shocked. There were deep new lines at the corner of the Sheikh's eyes and when he smiled you could see that it was an effort.

'Major McDonald.' He held out his hand. 'Good of you to come. I need your help.'

He explained succinctly.

'I've had the sharpest private detectives that money can buy digging into it for six months. The woman has disappeared,' he concluded.

'No,' said the Major with quiet confidence, 'they have just not looked for her in the right way. You're sure she's English?'

'Yes.'

'Then let me use my contacts. I'll find her for you.'

Amer went to the window and looked out. The city street looked like a mineral maze in the spring sunshine. He said to the pavement below, 'If you find her, you bring the information straight to me. You don't tell her. Or anyone else.'

The Major was surprised into indiscretion. 'Are things so explosive in Dalmun, then?'

Amer turned back and smiled. It was not a pleasant smile. 'It is not Dalmun which is explosive,' he said in a matter-of-fact voice. 'It's me. This one is *mine*.'

The weekend with the Hartleys did not turn out as Leo expected. She thought it was going to be a relaxed, family affair, mowing lawns and cleaning swimming pools. She could not have been more wrong.

There was a dinner party on Friday night, when she and Claire got down there; a lunch party—'Just close friends, darling'—on Saturday; a sailing club dance on Saturday evening to which the entire household and their guest were expected to turn up; and a drinks party for over a hundred before lunch on Sunday. In between whiles Simon's mother, a cut-glass blonde, took her on a guided tour of the family pile. It was crumbling and, in Leo's view, badly in need of being turned into a conference centre. Simon's baronet father walked her through several acres of formal garden, equally neglected.

And Simon. Well, she did not know what Simon was doing at all. Except that he kept getting her on her own and telling her how well he got on with her father.

By Sunday afternoon, Leo was feeling breathless, uneasy and her wardrobe had given out.

'Shouldn't we be going back to London?' she whispered to Claire.

Lady Hartley, whose hearing would have roused envy in a bat, intervened.

'Simon, darling. You haven't shown Leo the river. Why don't you go now? You might see a kingfisher.'

'Who are the Kingfishers?' said Leo nervously.

Simon stood up, laughing. 'It's all right. The feathered kind. No more socialising, I promise.'

'Thank God for that,' said Leo.

'Is it like this every weekend?' she asked as they walked up the hill behind the house.

Simon shook his head. 'Mum wanted to make sure you had a good time.'

'Is that why I feel like I've been heavily marketed to?' Leo mused. She saw Simon's expression and said remorsefully, 'Oh I'm so sorry. That was a stupid thing to say. Of course your mother wasn't marketing. What would she be selling, after all?'

But Simon was a gentleman.

'Me, I'm afraid,' he said quietly.

Leo was deprived of speech.

Simon took her hand again and held it in a steady clasp.

'I won't pretend any nonsense, Leo. I respect you too much for that. Anyway, you'd see through it. The family fortunes have pretty much hit rock bottom, you see. The only way out is an injection of capital from—well—'

'Me,' said Leo. She still felt bewildered. 'Do they want to sell? I mean, I can see this place has potential. But would your parents really like to see it as part of the Groom Hotel chain? Anyway, they'd be better talking to my father or the Head of UK Operations than me.'

Simon looked down at their clasped hands. His expression was rueful.

'It's not the house they want to sell.' And as Leo still stared at him, brows knit in confusion, he said roughly, 'They want me to ask you to marry me.'

'What?'

Simon dropped her hand. 'There's no need to sound so shocked. You must have realised.'

'I—' Leo felt a fool. What was it Amer had said? *You don't know how to play this game, do you?* Oh boy, was he right. 'I'm sorry,' she said quietly. 'I didn't know.'

Simon looked wretched. 'I thought at least your father would have hinted...'

'My father—?'

And then she saw, quite suddenly, what it was all about. Why Gordon Groom had brought Simon to Cairo; why her mother had asked about her feelings for him all those months ago; why ever since she got back she had been pushing files around her office trying to find the job that her father assured her was there.

Fool. Fool. *Double* fool. If you want a son and heir and all you have is an ugly duckling daughter, buy her an amenable husband and go for the next generation.

'There never was a career for me at Grooms, was there?'

said Leo. She was not talking to Simon. 'It was just to keep me quiet until I got married.' She did not know which was worse, the hurt or the humiliation.

Simon did not seem to notice. He nodded, relieved. 'Will you?'

She wanted to scream. She wanted to cry. She wanted to rage at the Heavens. She wanted to tell her father exactly what she thought of him before stamping out of his house and his nonjob.

But none of that was Simon's fault and Leo was fair minded to a fault.

'No, I won't marry you,' she said quite gently.

Simon was taken aback. After all, thought Leo savagely, he worked for Gordon Groom, too.

'I won't give up hope,' he assured her kindly.

And then she did scream.

'Well,' said Amer in quiet satisfaction, 'you said you'd do it and you have. I'm impressed.'

Major McDonald shrugged. 'I put my team on it. The statistician pointed out that Leonora is so unusual it doesn't even get recorded in most profiles of first names. Add that bit of information to someone who was able to hide her identity from the start of her arrival in Cairo, and you've got a spy, a criminal or an offspring of the seriously rich. Fortunately for you, she is the latter.'

'Fortunate indeed,' agreed Amer affably.

He showed his teeth in a smile that made the Major wonder what Leonora Groom had done. He liked and admired Amer but, just for a moment, he felt almost sorry for the woman.

Amer flipped open the file.

'Leonora Groom,' he said. He rolled it round his mouth like a fine wine. 'Leonora Groom.'

'There's only one picture,' the Major pointed out. 'At the Antika opening. She seems to keep out of the photographers' way, even at these charity receptions. It's almost as if she wants to stay anonymous.'

'As you say,' Amer agreed suavely.

He was very angry. How dared she lie to him? She had strung him along like some negligible tourist.

A small voice reminded him that he had been less than candid with her, too. He had not even told her his full name, after all. He ignored it and closed the dossier decisively.

'Hari will settle your account. Goodbye and thank you.'

Hari handed over a substantial cheque and showed the Major out. He came back to Amer. He was surprised to find that he was bent over his desk writing fast and he did not like the look of his friend's expression at all.

'What are you going to do?' he said in trepidation.

Amer narrowed his eyes at the paper in front of him. He gave a soft laugh. It made Hari's blood run cold.

'Need you ask? Make her come to me, of course.'

Leo intended to have the whole thing out with her father as soon as she got back. Only she had forgotten that he was away on an extended trip trying to rescue his Far East operation. In his absence it almost seemed as if she had a real job after all.

So she stayed.

May came, sending long tendrils of engulfing wisteria all over the front of the Wimbledon house. In the morning Leo sniffed the heady scent in pure pleasure. But at night, in the dark, it recalled another night, when you could see the stars and the only scent was a man's skin and unfamiliar cologne. She would remember that cologne for ever.

'Don't think about him,' she told herself fiercely. 'Just—don't—*think*.'

But it was not easy with Simon calling regularly, pointing out that she liked him—didn't she?—and she wasn't committed to anybody else. He did not phrase that, Leo noted wryly, as a question. And anyway, she could hardly say that she was haunted by the shadow of a man whose body never touched hers.

In the effort of not thinking about that, Leo ripped through all the work she could find and looked around for more. This turn of events terrorised her secretary to such an extent that when a cardboard parcel arrived by courier, Joanne rushed it into her office as if it was a communication from Mars.

Leo considered it without interest. 'Looks like a souvenir programme of some sort,' she said indifferently.

'But *biked over*,' said Joanne, impressed.

Leo shrugged.

'Okay. Open up and see what it is.'

But Joanne was doomed to disappointment. 'It's just that book of essays the Antika Project were putting together. Mr Groom got one of the PR writers to do it for him.' She flicked through the index. 'Yes here it is. "Gordon Groom on how to ruin a hotel." It was funny.'

Leo was mildly interested. Her father was not noted for his sense of humour.

'That's what they asked for,' explained Joanne. 'Everyone was supposed to write a piece sending themselves up.' She ran her finger down the index. '"Food Poisonous Food" by the Chef of the Year. "Come With Me To The Casbah" by Sheikh Amer el-Barbary. "Heartthrobs Don't Get Measles" by Jeremy Derringer.' She looked up. 'What?'

'Run that by me again,' said Leo. She was very pale, suddenly.

'"Heartthrobs Don't Get Measles"', said Joanne obligingly. 'Do you know Jeremy Derringer then? Gosh, he's gorgeous.'

Leo did not answer. She put out a shaking hand for the book. Joanne gave it to her. Leo did not even notice when Joanne left the room.

Amer had enjoyed writing the article. He had started it in a white hot rage with Leo. How dared she challenge him like that when all the time she knew she was deceiving him about her identity? And then to run away, covering her tracks so totally that he had the devil's own job to find her! She knew he had intended to see her again. How dared she disappear, without so much as a word of regret? He was going to bring her back on her *knees*.

But then, as he wrote, Amer's fury began to dissipate in sheer amusement. He finished it at a tearing rate. Then he sent it off before he could have second thoughts.

Leo, of course, did not know that. But she did know Amer. As she read, she could hear his gleeful voice. That arrogant cynicism stretched a mocking arm off the printed page and tweaked her nose until tears started.

"Rudolf Valentino has much to answer for," Amer had written enjoyably. "He gave women what they wanted. Then said it was to be found in men of the desert. For those of us who carry this terrible responsibility, I suggest a few tips."

What followed was a precise outline of his strategy for their evening together. He had forgotten nothing. Not lifting her into the boat. Not her reluctant capitulation to the comfort of the cushions. Not putting his jacket round her shoulders. Leo shivered to remember it. That made her even more furious. Not—oh God, her heart beat in an agony of shame as she remembered—her mesmerised unsophistication.

'You really don't know how to play this game, do you?' he had said. And there it was in black and white.

"Never forget you are taking them on an exotic journey through their own fantasies."

'Oh *no*,' moaned Leo.

"Stay in charge. They will accept any rules you lay down, however lunatic. It is what they secretly want. Only they cannot bear to admit it."

Leo put the article down. 'I'll kill him,' she said aloud. For a moment she could almost believe she meant it.

She flung the book so hard across the room that its spine split. *Good,* thought Leo. She was shaking and very cold. She felt as if he had stripped her publicly.

How many women had he taken on his Nile fantasy? she thought savagely. How many had he looked at in that way until they started to shake with tension? While all the time he was laughing at them.

Leo hugged her arms round herself protectively. It was like the worst of her adolescence, all over again. The painfully acquired assurance counted for nothing. Suddenly she was awkward, clumsy, unsubtle and plain. No man would look at her, ever.

Except Simon. He might not be in love with her, but he liked her. He even respected her, for God's sake. And he was honest about it.

Leo picked up the phone.

Amer took breakfast in the conservatory of his Mayfair house. He basked in the warmth of sun filtering through glass, while he sipped orange juice and leafed through the morning papers. He was not, he assured himself, waiting for anything. Just because Leo would have had the booklet with his article in it four days ago was no reason to stretch his ears for the burr of the telephone.

Still, the Embassy had been briefed that Miss Groom was, exceptionally, to be given his private London number. And no one could say that the papers were gripping. Amer reached the 'Forthcoming Marriages' column without interest and was on the point of turning that page, too, when—

The crystal glass fell from his hand, scattering shards and orange juice all over the marble floor.

She could not have done it; she was not stupid. She *could* not.

But it was there. Irrefutably. "Leonora Jane, only daughter of Gordon Groom of the Wisteria House Wimbledon and Mrs Deborah Groom of Kensington, W8 to Mr Simon Hartley, eldest son of Sir Donald and Lady Hartley of Seren Place, Devon."

She had got herself engaged.

'I'll kill her,' yelled Amer.

CHAPTER FIVE

LEO rang her father in Singapore to tell him that she and Simon were engaged. Gordon Groom's reaction startled her.

'At last.'

'Excuse me?'

'It's taken you long enough. Still, he's a good lad and I'm pleased.'

Why did it sound like the approval he used to dole out when she came home with a good school report?

'Thank you for your good wishes,' said Leo drily.

'I'm going into a meeting. Tell Hartley I'll call him tomorrow eight o' clock UK time.' He rang off.

'Yes, I'm sure we'll be very happy,' Leo said to the buzzing phone. She flung it back onto its stand and attacked her In box as if it was a personal enemy.

Maybe her mother would react more normally, when they had their girls' lunch, she thought.

But, unlike Gordon, Deborah disapproved and made no bones about it.

'You can't fool me,' Deborah announced. She knocked back a gin and tonic as if it was medicine. 'This is your father's doing.'

Leo shook her head. 'Pops hasn't done anything. Simon asked me to marry him. I said yes. That's all. I did think about it first, Ma.'

Deborah looked at her with tragic eyes. She had just come from a whole morning at her favourite Bond Street beautician and her exquisite make-up enhanced the tragic vulnerability. Leo's feet felt like boats. Under the table, she shuffled them. Her mother took no notice.

'Think,' she said dramatically. 'If you're in love you don't

73

think. You just *fly*.' Her gloved hands made a large gesture similar to a plant bursting into flower.

It was all too reminiscent of childhood dance classes. Leo looked over her shoulder to check that no passing waiter had had to dodge Deborah's expressiveness.

'Come on, Ma. Keep the music and movement down.'

Deborah blinked the long silky lashes which were the only feature she had bequeathed to her daughter.

'You're laughing at me. You don't know how serious this is.'

'I take getting married very seriously,' Leo said stiffly.

Deborah ignored that. 'Have you been to bed with him yet?'

'*Mother!*'

'I thought not,' said Deborah, pleased with herself. 'Don't you think that's odd? If he is in love with you, I mean.'

'He's not in love with me,' Leo said quietly.

That stopped Deborah as nothing else would have done. 'Oh, Leo. Oh, darling.'

'Ma, you're barking up the wrong tree.' Leo leaned forward and spoke earnestly. 'It really was my decision. Simon doesn't love me and I don't love him. But we have a lot in common. It will work out.'

Deborah looked as if she was going to cry.

Leo thought desperately for something to reassure her. 'He tells me the truth.'

It did not have the effect she expected. Her mother sat bolt upright.

'Tells you the truth?'

'Yes.'

'The truth about what?'

It was unexpected. Leo floundered. 'Well who he is. What he feels. What he wants.'

Deborah put her head on one side. 'So who doesn't?'

Leo was scornful. 'Oh come on, Ma. You know more about men than I do. You know they play games. Tie you up in knots. And not one damn thing they tell you is true.'

She stopped. She realised that Deborah's eyes were uncomfortably shrewd.

'Are we talking about the man who told you to grow your hair?' her mother asked interestedly.

Leo could have thrown something. 'What do you mean?'

'You've cut your hair like a space helmet for years. Then suddenly it's on your shoulders. Looks good, too. So someone has been giving you style advice. Who is he?'

Leo tensed. 'No one. You're imagining it, Ma.'

She spoke more curtly than she meant to. Deborah's eyebrows flew up. Leo was never curt with her.

'He hurt you,' she said on a note of discovery.

'Nonsense.'

Deborah ignored that. 'Darling, we all get hurt sometimes. Men,' she said largely, 'don't *think*. That doesn't mean...'

But Leo was not listening. She gave a harsh laugh.

'Some of them think. Some of them think a whole lot. In fact, they have a tried and trusted plan of campaign ready for use on any woman they come across.'

Deborah stared. 'But—'

'*Any* woman,' Leo said with emphasis.

'Oh, darling,' said Deborah with compunction, 'you haven't fallen for a Don Juan? Not you?'

'I haven't fallen for anyone,' said Leo furiously. 'And I'm not going to.'

'Well, lucky old Simon,' said Deborah.

None of which sent Leo back to the office any happier. She was still fuming when she sat down and applied herself to her e-mail. Almost at once she found a name that added fuel to the fire.

Quickly she paged through the list of the day's callers. He had called again. And again. And—

She buzzed Joanne.

'I'm looking at my message list. Tell me about Sheikh el-Barbary. What did he want?'

Amer was in a cold rage.

'Are you telling me she won't take my call?' he demanded.

Hari shrugged. He was puzzled by this excitement over a woman he had never heard of.

'The secretary claims Miss Groom is not in the office.'

'I don't believe it.'

Hari started to shrug again. Then caught sight of Amer's steely expression and thought better of it.

'The switchboard operator said she has just announced her engagement. They have been swamped with calls of congratulation this morning, apparently,' he offered placatingly.

'I am not,' said Amer between his teeth, 'offering my congratulations. What the hell is she doing?'

'Out choosing the ring, I expect,' said Hari crisply.

He encountered a look that startled him.

'Who is this woman?' he demanded, shaken.

Amer picked up Major McDonald's file and flung it at him. Hari picked it up and started to leaf through it curiously. Amer paced the floor, his shoulders hunched.

Hari finished reading and looked up. 'Leonora Roberts? Your mystery lady in Cairo is the Groom heiress?'

'Quite,' snarled Amer.

'Well, she sure didn't behave like an heiress,' said Hari, astonished.

Amer stopped pacing. 'No, she didn't did she?' he said in an arrested voice. 'I wonder—' He made a decision. 'Call the woman again.'

'But she is out.'

'Not Leonora Groom,' said Amer impatiently. 'The secretary. I want to know if she has read the Antika Project's Celebrity Essays.'

Hari suddenly understood. 'You sent her that?' he gasped. 'Twenty Ways to Catch a Woman by the last of the Ladykillers? You must be out of your mind. She'll never speak to you again.'

Amer strode to the window. The cherry trees in the garden were coming to the end of their blossom. He stared at them unseeingly.

'She will,' he said in a low voice. 'If I have to kidnap her and lock her up to do it, I'll make her listen to me.'

Hari looked dubious but he made the call.

Amer rested his brow against the window-pane. His temples throbbed. He should never have let her get away that night in Cairo. She had been so nearly his. He was experienced enough to know that if he had just put out a hand and touched her she would have gone with him wherever he said. She was too unsophisticated to hide her feelings. Maybe even too inexperienced to recognise them. But Amer had recognised them all right. He could have done whatever he wanted with her that night.

But he had wanted— Well what had he wanted? He asked himself now, with bitter irony. Whatever it was, he had had six months to regret that he had not taken what was in his hands.

He was not, Amer promised himself, going to let that happen again. The next time he got his hands on Leonora Groom, she was not getting away until he got what he wanted. Whatever it was.

Hari put the phone down. 'She has read it,' he said in a voice of doom. 'Her secretary was quite sure of that. Because it was immediately after she left Miss Groom reading it that she called Mr Hartley. That was when they got engaged.'

There was a disbelieving silence. Then Amer swore.

He had dared to call her! Leo's first flare of rage turned into something more complicated. She was honest enough to admit that it was largely excitement.

What sort of person, am I? she thought, horrified. Engaged to one man, getting goose bumps when another man calls me!

She tried to talk to Simon. His office said he was visiting the Birmingham hotel.

'Oh,' said Leo disconcerted. She had expected to go on the Midlands trip. 'Oh well, I suppose it isn't urgent.'

But somehow it felt urgent. She moved about her office

restlessly. There were three applications in her In box but she just could not *concentrate*.

Joanne buzzed.

'The front hall rang up to say your car is ready when you are.' There was a faint question mark in her tone.

Leo chuckled. 'Conscience car. Simon knows he should have taken me to Birmingham, too.'

'I expect he thought you had other things to do.' To her surprise Joanne sounded uncomfortable. 'Shall I lock up for you?'

'I suppose so,' said Leo, dissatisfied. 'It's been a messy day. Maybe I'll do better if I take some work home.'

Fifteen minutes later she was running down the steps of the Groom building, a portfolio under one arm a substantial brief-case in the other and her handbag looped over one shoulder. She went straight to the parking space reserved for Board members. A uniformed man leaped out and opened the door for her.

'Hi,' said Leo, surprised. 'Darren got the day off?'

But the man just smiled and took the portfolio and brief-case from her. She sank into the seat and stretched her legs out. It was a shock. Her feet came nowhere near the back of the seat in front. Even her father did not demand this degree of luxury.

She became aware of a still presence beside her just as the chauffeur started the engine.

'Good evening, Leonora,' said a voice out of her dreams.

Out of her dreams. Out of her nightmares. Out of her sleepless nights. Leo went hot, cold, then deathly still.

The limousine eased silently through the gates and out into the rush hour traffic.

Leo said, 'What are you doing here?' Her frozen lips barely moved.

'Talking some sense into you before you do something neither of us will be able to put right,' said Amer with commendable honesty but a certain lack of tact.

'Let me out of this car.'

He gave a soft laugh. How she hated that laugh. It sounded gloating. It also made those goose bumps break out up and down her spine again.

'You don't mean that,' he said confidently.

Leo pulled herself together. 'You know I do. This is kidnapping,' she pointed out.

He waved that aside. 'There was no time for the courtesies. I needed to see you urgently.'

The car was gliding through the traffic at a fair speed. Leo discarded the thought of leaping out. So she did the next best thing. She crossed her legs, leaned back into the aromatic softness of leather and looked at Amer with all the mockery she could muster.

'Really?' she said politely. 'Six months, is it? Seven? Urgent indeed.'

Amer's mouth compressed. 'You covered your tracks well.'

Leo bit back a smug smile. 'I wasn't aware I had covered my tracks at all,' she said airily.

'False name. Phoney job. No forwarding address. No continuing friendships. My enquiries met stone wall after stone wall.'

'Enquiries?' Leo slewed round in her seat, smugness evaporating. 'Are you saying you put a private detective on to me?'

She was furious. But she felt oddly excited as well. So he had not just let her walk away without a thought. She had imagined Amer giving a philosophical shrug at the escape of one insignificant girl and turning to the next one.

Amer waved that aside as well. 'I wanted to find you,' he said as if that justified anything.

'Oh well, that's all right then,' said Leo affably. She was shaking with rage. And other things which she was not thinking about at the moment. 'Whatever the Sheikh wants he gets, right? Never mind what anyone else wants.'

He smiled. 'You've grown your hair.'

Leo was so angry she did not even blush. She drummed her clenched fists on her knees in frustration.

'It suits you. I knew it would.'

'Stop this car. Let me out at once.'

'Don't panic. I'm taking you home,' he said soothingly.

'I am not panicking,' said Leo between her teeth. 'And I don't want to go home. I'm supposed to go to a reception at the National Gallery.'

'You work too hard. Your secretary can apologise for you tomorrow.'

'Ah. The Sheikh wants again, huh?'

He laughed suddenly. 'Stop spitting at me, Leonora. What is one reception among so many? This is important. We have unfinished business and we both know it.'

'I'm engaged,' said Leo harshly.

She wished she had the ring on her finger to prove it. But she and Simon had not yet taken the time to choose one.

Amer smiled tolerantly. 'Yes, that's one of the things I want to talk about.'

Leo slewed round, her eyes wide with outrage. 'Excuse me?'

He leaned back in his corner and gave her that slow, sexy smile. Why had she only remembered that it set her heart pounding and not that it annoyed her to screaming point?

'It was very silly to get engaged just to spite me,' he said indulgently.

'What?'

'You weren't engaged before I hit town.'

'Coincidence,' said Leo curtly. Her heart was beating so hard she thought he must be able to hear it.

'Was it coincidence that you read my piece in that charity book and got engaged immediately afterwards?' he asked shrewdly.

'How did you know—?' Leo broke off. But it was too late. She bit her lip.

'A very understandable reaction,' Amer assured her kindly.

'I have read the thing again and I admit I went over the top in a couple of places. But—'

'Over the top?' Leo glared at him. 'Oh I wouldn't say that. I think you got it all pretty accurately. At least from what I remember. But you should check with your other victims.'

'Victims?' That startled him, genuinely.

'Targets then,' said Leo, showing her teeth. 'How does that sound?'

'Calculating,' Amer said slowly.

She gave him a wide, false smile. 'I couldn't have put it better myself.'

He said on a note of discovery, 'Was *that* why you got engaged then? Because you thought I was playing games with you?'

'Are you trying to tell me you weren't playing games?' Leo looked at him with ineffable scorn. 'That heavily stage-managed incident in Cairo was all leading to love, marriage and a lifetime's devotion, was it?'

Amer frowned. 'I don't know where it was leading,' he said shortly. 'You didn't give us time to find out.'

'But marriage was on the cards?' pressed Leo, mocking.

There was a pause. Then, 'No,' Amer admitted heavily.

'The truth at last,' Leo said with contempt. 'So face it and get out of my life.' She leaned forward and tapped the chauffeur on the shoulder. 'Trafalgar Square, the National Gallery Sainsbury wing. His Excellency made a mistake. I've got a reception to go to.'

The man looked in the driving mirror for instruction. Amer's expression was masklike. He nodded.

Leo had a tough week. Her father and Simon seemed to be talking to each other but they only left one message a piece on her answering machine. Which left far too much time to think about Amer el-Barbary.

Especially as he did not call her. Of course she would not have talked to him, if he had, Leo assured herself. She read his outrageous essay again to remind herself exactly why. She read it several times.

After Simon's message, an exclusive jeweller brought round a selection of engagement rings for her to try. Leo recognised the logo. It was a shop her father used regularly. Disturbed, she chose a ring almost at random.

If Amer had rung then, she would have talked to him. He did not. Just as well, Leo told herself.

Instead she had to give an interview to a magazine. Leo always shied away from personal publicity. But this time the journalist was a friend of Simon's and he had asked her to do it as a favour.

So Anne Marie Dance of *Finance Today* came to interview her. Only she did not behave like a friend of anyone. She went on the attack at once.

'How does it feel to work in your father's shadow all the time?'

It was not the first time she had been asked that one, though the woman's hostility was a shock.

After a moment she said in her driest tone, 'Educational.'

Anne Marie nodded, as if a worthy opponent had scored a point. But not won the game. She leaned forward.

'It won't happen you know.'

Leo said blankly, 'I'm sorry?'

'You won't take over Grooms. Has your father ever appointed a woman director? A senior manager, even? Why do you think he brought Simon Hartley on board?'

Leo gave her a tolerant smile. 'Come on, Ms Dance. You know the rules. Happy to talk about the business. My private life is off limits.'

The journalist raised an eyebrow. 'So what's private about your life?'

Leo stiffened.

At once the woman said, 'I'm sorry. I shouldn't have said that. Is it all right if I ask whether the el-Barbarys are going to take a stake in Grooms?'

For the first time in the interview, Leo lost her professional poker face and she knew it.

'What makes you say that?' she demanded, trying to recover.

Anne Marie Dance's smile was faintly malicious.

'Surely you know the el-Barbarys? Oil? Minerals? Race horses?' The journalist was impatient. 'Ever since the oil boom they've been buying up large chunks of western industry.'

Leo's brain worked swiftly. Amer was using the company to get at her. Or he was using her to get at the company; a nasty thought that. Alternatively he was not interested in the company at all but he had been asking about her and the journalist misinterpreted.

'What makes you think they are looking at Grooms?' Leo asked carefully.

But the journalist just laughed. 'You can't expect me to tell you that, Ms Groom. Got to protect my sources. Let's just say—they have been showing an interest.'

She snapped her notebook shut and got up to leave. Leo escorted her to the lift. As she held out her hand to say goodbye, the journalist looked down at it almost with compassion. Disconcerted, Leo looked down. And there it was, the characteristic ink stain, half-way down her middle finger. She stuffed her hand into her pocket but it was too late.

'Goodbye, Ms Groom. Good luck.' She almost sounded as if she meant it. It was disturbing.

Leo almost ran back to her office. Her secretary looked up surprised.

'No rush. The reception doesn't start until six. Plenty of time to get to the Science Museum.' She added in sudden concern, 'Have you hurt your hand?'

Reluctantly Leo brought it out of her pocket. She shrugged, mocking herself.

'No. It's just the ink stain on the right doesn't really go with the rose diamond on the left.'

'What you need,' said Joanne comfortably, 'is a shower. Thank God for a decent ladies' room.'

'I don't think this is a very good idea.' Hari was beginning to feel seriously alarmed. 'I mean what's she going to do? You know what women are. False pretences. Sexual harassment. They can get crazy.'

Amer shrugged.

'Think of the scandal,' moaned Hari. 'After all the trouble you took to set up a meeting with the disaffected tribes. It's a risk we don't need.'

Amer's mouth set. 'I must see her. I am going to see her.'

'I don't know what's happened to you. I've never seen you like this.'

The dark grey eyes were suddenly, startlingly, intense.

'Maybe you've never seen me a hundred per cent alive before.'

Hari gave up.

Leo took her toilet bag and cocktail dress and went along to change. A couple of women were already there, repairing their make-up and chatting about their love lives.

'Clever men are hell, aren't they?' one of them told the mirror. She arched a friendly eyebrow, including Leo in the conversation.

Leo smiled but her voice was resigned when she said 'Try me on corporate recognition. Better still, high season occupancy rates. I'm the bees' knees at that. Men—clever or not—are a closed book to me.'

The pretty painted face in the mirror looked almost pitying for a moment. 'Join the club.'

She's sorry for me, thought Leo. That makes the second woman this afternoon. What a complete disaster I must be. And they only have to look at me to see it. It was a shocking thought.

The others left and she went into the tiny shower room.

Leo slid out of her clothes and turned on the shower. She felt numb. Automatically she applied her favourite shower gel. It was her one extravagance, specially imported from Japan. It made her skin soft as silk under her fingers and perfumed her whole body with the faint but lingering scent of spring blossom. Slowly, slowly, she began to feel again.

What she felt was anger. And suddenly, blessedly, ready to fight back.

How dared her father treat her like a cipher? Stick her in a nonjob and then stop speaking to her altogether as soon as she got engaged to the man of his choice! How dared Simon send her a mail-order engagement ring?

Above all, how dared Amer el-Barbary virtually kidnap her in his blasted limousine and then leave her without a word for over a week?

By the time Leo was dressed in designer black, with her newly washed hair piled on top of her head, she was glittering with the hunger for battle.

She glared at herself in the mirror and said violently, '*Bloody* men.'

The stunned look had gone but she was still too pale. Leo shook herself. This would never do. She had just got engaged, for Heaven's sake. Until she took charge of her own life and dealt with the men who had sewn her up she had to look *radiant.*

She made an inventory of her attractions. There were not many of them. But at least you could not see her big feet in the waist-high mirror, Leo thought wryly. Otherwise there was her porcelain skin, her embarrassingly voluptuous figure and a very expensive dress. That was it.

It was why all these men thought they could push her around to fit in with their plans. If she had been attractive, they would have thought about what was good for her. What she wanted; *listened* to her. As it was—Leo ground her teeth.

It made a mess of her make-up. She had to wipe off her lipstick and start again. That did not do much for her mood, either.

'Now calm down,' she said to herself. 'You can do make-up.'

At Christmas Deborah had given her a voucher for a whole day's beauty treatment. Leo had bought most of the cosmetics the make-up artist pressed on her, out of sheer self-defence. Now, she thought with acute self-mockery, all she had to do was remember which colour went where.

She remembered. Ten minutes later she hardly recognised the face that looked back at her. Slumberous eyes, startlingly long lashes, provocative mouth... At least no one is going to feel sorry for me tonight, Leo thought with a flare of savage satisfaction.

And as for her dress—she considered it clinically. It was low-cut and very plain, designed to show off her creamy shoulders. Well that was all right but—Leo wriggled it down further to accentuate the effect. Only that deepened the décolletage. Oh well, thought Leo, valiant with fury, why not?

She threw a brilliant embroidered shawl over her dress and stalked down to the car. On the way she noticed her right hand. Despite the shower the shadow of the ink stain on the middle finger was still visible.

'Damn,' spat Leo.

She dabbed at her finger with a tissue. And felt the spring which controlled her temper tighten another notch.

It did not show when she arrived at the Museum. She stepped out as haughtily as a queen. Or so thought Hari, who had been left on watch for her.

'Whoops,' he said under his breath.

He had only seen Leo once before and she had changed beyond belief. But he knew the signs. This was not a woman in the mood for romantic abduction. This was a woman who was in a mood to kill.

He went to warn Amer.

Leo accepted a glass of champagne from one of the Foundation's officials and allowed herself to be guided through a rather dull display of the Foundation's recent achievements. They all looked taken aback at this dramatic new Leo. Even

Professor Lane stumbled in his monologue and one or two of the students looked as nervous as they were admiring.

Good, she thought savagely. She downed her first glass and took another one.

She circulated grimly, skirting an early sewing machine, and pointing out crisply to Antika's Project Director that his business plan needed to be completely rewritten. He was sweating faintly by the time she turned away to inspect a large steam train.

'Whew,' said the Project Director, wiping his brow.

He went to look for reinforcements.

Leo hid a smile. At least that was one man who would take her seriously from now on. Feeling better and better, she took a third glass of champagne from a passing waiter. And then, from behind the huge engine, came a voice she thought she recognised.

'Tell her,' it said urgently. 'Tell her *now.*'

Leo's brow creased. Someone from work? No. Yet someone she had talked to today. A business contact? No. Then, suddenly, she had it—the unfriendly journalist. That was who it was. What was her name?

A man's voice muttered a reply. Indistinguishable.

'You can't do it,' said the journalist. She sounded on the edge of hysteria. 'It's crazy. Your whole life.'

'Anne Marie, don't. Not here. *Please.*'

Anne Marie Dance. Of course. And the man sounded desperate. Leo was about to back away tactfully when she heard the thing that stopped her dead in her tracks.

'Simon, you can't *do* this.'

Simon?

Simon?

She put her untasted glass down on the priceless exhibit and walked quite deliberately round the steam engine. Simon Hartley was standing there, holding Anne Marie Dance at arm's length. Leo stopped dead, all her bright triumph draining out of her. At arm's length, yes. But what intimacy there was in their closeness. They had obviously been closer than this many many times.

Anne Marie saw her over Simon's shoulder. Her face changed. Simon turned round. When he saw Leo he looked blank, then horribly sick.

'Oh God,' he said.

Anne Marie Dance, on the other hand, seemed almost relieved. Quite suddenly Leo realised why there had been that inexplicable hostility in the interview this afternoon.

'So now you know,' she said.

She put a possessive hand on Simon's arm. After a moment his hand covered hers protectively. As if he had made that gesture a hundred times before.

Leo felt as if a knife had gone into her heart, straight and true. Not because she wanted Simon, but because no one was ever going to touch her with that instinctive protectiveness. She blinked hard.

'Leo, I'm so sorry,' he said wretchedly.

'I'm not,' said Anne Marie in a quick panting voice. 'It's time someone showed your father there are things he can't buy. Like a son-in-law.'

Simon dropped her hand as if it burned him.

'Stop it, Anne Marie,' he said, suddenly taking charge. 'Leo, we can't talk here.'

'Why not?' said Anne Marie loudly. She shouldered her way round him and stuck her face close to Leo's. 'Your father told Simon to propose to you. He said you wanted to marry and couldn't get a man of your own.'

Leo felt as if she were in a nightmare. All the lovely defiance had evaporated. She felt cold and alone. Anne Marie's hostility hurt. But at least it was better than the pity that had followed it last time.

She said in a voice like crashing icebergs, 'He was wrong.'

She tugged at the newly acquired rose diamond with clumsy fingers. Even though she had put it on so recently it was difficult to prize off.

'Not here,' implored Simon, looking round anxiously.

But they were out of sight of most other people in the gallery. Leo set her teeth and hauled. Her finger turned white, then red. But in the end the thing came off. She dropped it into his top pocket.

'Don't worry. I'll tell Gordon I changed my mind,' she told him, still in that frighteningly icy voice.

She knew she should be devastated by Simon's betrayal. No doubt she would be when she had time to think about it. But for the moment she still felt blessedly numb. The worst thing was the humiliation. And if she kept a hold on herself and got out fast, she could even handle that, Leo told herself.

'He won't sack you if he thinks it's my fault.'

Simon flinched. That was faintly satisfying. She gathered herself to leave them.

'I'll send a cancellation notice to the papers tomorrow.'

Simon flushed. Leo thought—how could I have imagined it would work? How could I have *trusted* him? He's as bad as Amer el-Barbary.

She said with absolute finality, 'Goodbye.'

Out of the shelter of the great locomotive, Leo felt suddenly exposed. She went through the galleries as fast as she could without actually appearing to be running. All she wanted to do now was get home.

She was so nearly out of the door when she heard her name called that she could have screamed.

'Leonora!'

She whirled round. Sheikh Amer el-Barbary strolled forward. A scream, she decided, did not begin to cover what she felt.

'Hello to the end of a perfect day,' she said.

He was heart-stoppingly handsome, with his golden tan that she remembered—and lazy eyes which she had tried so hard to forget. Tonight they looked almost silver. In the flesh he was incredibly sexy. How had she managed to get by last week without reacting to it? She looked at him with acute dislike.

'What do you want?'

Amer's eyebrows flew up at her abrupt tone.

'How many of those have you had?' he asked, nodding at the champagne.

Leo ignored the question. 'I have not come here to talk to you. Go away.'

She waved her glass to emphasis her point. Some of the wine spilled over his immaculate grey suit. She ignored that, too.

'I see,' he said gravely.

He took her by the arm and steered her to a corner of the room. Hari hovered. Amer waved him away. He went.

Leo's dislike of Sheikh Amer el-Barbary intensified. She did not attempt to disguise it.

'And you needn't think you can order me around, either,' she said pugnaciously. 'That little man may be paid to hit the ceiling when you say jump. I'm not.'

'Quite right,' said Amer hugely entertained. 'But I really do have something to discuss with you. Business,' he added, as her eyes flashed.

'What business?' demanded Leo, suspicious.

'Antika's research. I gather you don't like the application.'

Leo pulled herself together and told him succinctly exactly what was wrong with the application. Amer blinked.

'No wonder you frightened the poor guy to death,' he murmured. 'Now, how can I resolve your criticisms?'

'What has it got to do with you?' Leo said, bristling.

'We are co-funding it.' He was smoothness itself. 'Professor Lane has asked me to see what I can do.'

His voice was like a caress. The faint accent and overprecise English added to the illusion. Many women, thought Leo wisely, would have melted into a warm puddle at his feet when he stroked them with that voice. On the Nile, she had nearly done exactly that herself.

She glared. Amer gave her a wide smile that showed perfect teeth and an indentation in one cheek that many women would have found irresistible. Leo thanked God she was not many women. She took a gulp of champagne.

'I don't believe it,' she said.

He was amused. 'How do I convince you?'

Leo eyed him over the top of her champagne glass. She was shaking with temper and more than temper. Suddenly a crazy stratagem presented itself. It would make him mad but it was irresistible. Anyway, Leo wasn't going to resist, not in the mood she was in tonight.

She gave him a wide smile and said with profoundly phoney calm, 'Okay. You believe in Antika's research. I don't. So carry on. Pitch.'

He was taken aback. Leo saw it. She savoured it. It did not make up for the humiliations of the day, of course. but it helped. It helped.

The caressing note faltered. 'Excuse me?'

'Pitch,' she said. She clicked her fingers impatiently. 'Give me your line.'

It was insulting. Amer stiffened. She eyed him with mockery.

'You have got a line, haven't you?'

'I don't think—'

Leo interrupted. 'No line? Fine.' She turned away. 'I'll be going. If you'll call my car—'

Amer stepped swiftly in front of her.

'I'll think of a line,' he said rapidly. 'Just give me a second.'

A hint of a caress now, Leo thought with satisfaction. Quite suddenly the Sheikh seemed to have dropped out of seduction mode and was prepared to do business. She began to feel triumphant at last.

Vaingloriously she drained her glass. Amer eyed the empty flute uneasily.

'How many *have* you had?'

'Enough,' said Leo.

He laughed suddenly. 'You're not at all what I thought you were in Cairo, you know.'

Leo blinked. 'What?'

He made a graceful gesture. He had beautiful hands, she

saw. Like a musician. Or a dancer. Or—the thought flipped
into her brain like an acrobat—a snake charmer.

'What?' she said again, challenging him.

'Jack Lane got you wrong, too. He said you were a nice,
quiet lady.' He sounded rueful. 'Not a fire eater in traffic
light silks.'

Leo hugged the maligned shawl round her. 'You want to
do business, I'll do business,' she said stubbornly.

'Excellent. Then maybe we could have dinner,' he said,
smooth as cream. 'Then I can take you through the proposal.'

'I've been through the proposal,' said Leo, standing her
ground. 'It's tosh.'

He did not like that. His eyes lost some of their laziness.
After a moment he said kindly, 'It's probably a little difficult
for a nonspecialist to follow. I would be happy to talk you
through—I'm sorry?'

'I said, garbage,' explained Leo.

His eyes flashed. 'It is a visionary project—'

'So it may be,' said Leo, interrupting. 'It's a damned
sloppy presentation.' She took a step towards him and prodded him in the chest with one finger to emphasise her point.
'I may not be a scientist with half a dozen degrees but I know
how to read a business plan. That one stinks.'

Amer looked down at her as if he could not believe his
ears. Well, he probably could not. She was vaguely aware
that he would not be used to women prodding him in the
chest. At least not in anger.

I am probably the only person in the world who sees him
for what he is, Leo thought, somewhat muzzily. A snake
charmer who thinks he can get anything he wants by mes-
merising people. She prodded him in the chest again.

'Facts,' she said. 'You want me to give these guys a sponsorship deal? Give me facts.'

Amer sighed. 'If they had any facts, the research would be
over and they wouldn't need a grant.'

Leo frowned, thinking about it. To her annoyance, it

sounded reasonable. Even spitting mad, she was fair minded enough to admit it.

'Okay. Hypotherase—' It got lost somehow. Leo tried again. 'Hypathetho—'

'Hypothesise,' he suggested helpfully.

Leo nodded. She raised her hand. Quick as an arrow, Amer caught her prodding finger before she could spear him for the third time. He was laughing, not lazily at all.

'No, please, not again. I will tell them to do as you suggest.'

'Good,' said Leo.

She found he was still holding her hand. She looked down at it, frowning in bewilderment.

'So now can we talk about us please?' he murmured.

He turned her hand over, studying it. That damned ink stain was still there. Leo swore and tugged her hand away. Without success.

'What do you mean—us?' she said nastily.

A long finger traced the ink stain thoughtfully.

'There is still that unfinished business.'

He looked up, provocatively. The dark eyes were teasing. But they were also surprisingly intense. Leo blinked.

'Isn't there?' he said softly.

And then he raised her hand to his mouth. He did not kiss it but held it where he could savour the feel and scent of her skin. He closed his eyes in appreciation.

As if, thought Leo wrathfully, her hand was a good cigar. She wrenched it out of his hold. He laughed, as if she had delighted him.

There was a nasty pause while Leo reminded herself that she was being played by a master. She controlled herself. It was an effort. Not helped by the fact that Amer was waiting for her next move with patent amusement.

At last she drew a long, shaky breath.

'Probably for the best,' said that hatefully appreciative voice.

Leo glared. 'What is?'

'Postponing our fight. You can't get up a really good head of steam when you're liable to be interrupted at any moment.'

'Our—' She choked. 'I do not,' she said with precision, 'fight.'

'Yes that's what I heard.' He sounded puzzled.

'And you're the last person in the world I would fight with if I did,' she raged.

That seemed to puzzle him even more.

'I'm sure you underrate yourself,' he said kindly.

For a wild moment Leo thought she was going to hit him. No, she thought. I won't. If I lose control, who knows where it will end?

She gathered her shawl around her and drew herself up to her full height.

'Good night.'

Amer interposed his shoulder, blocking her path. He smiled down at her.

'Why don't I take you out to dinner?'

Leo folded her lips together tightly before she could scream or burst into tears. She whipped round him, making for the front steps. To her consternation he followed.

'Surely we can negotiate.'

Leo increased her pace.

'I never negotiate.'

Even that did not put him off. 'But I do,' he said softly.

They were at the entrance. Leo stopped dead. She turned, head high.

'Okay,' she said in a goaded under voice. 'You want a deal? I'll give you a deal.'

She knew what she was going to say before it came out. It was crazy. Her better self did not want to have anything to do with this dark coda to the nightmare of the evening. But her better self was on hold, waiting for a cup of cocoa and a good cry in front of a blazing fire.

Her worse self was tired of being pushed around. Her worse self looked at his man and heard him admit that he pursued her cynically, knowing that marriage was not on the cards. Her worse self wanted revenge on the whole male sex.

Leo heard her worse self say in a hard voice, 'Marry me and I'll authorise that damned grant.'

CHAPTER SIX

THERE was a terrible silence.

Why on earth did I say that? I must be mad.

Then Amer threw back his head and laughed aloud. Leo could not believe it. She was still reeling with shock at her own words. And he *laughed*. At that moment she hated him.

But, even so, she needed to withdraw her stupid remark. And fast.

She said with stiff apology, 'That was uncalled for. I'm sorry. I didn't mean…'

Amer ignored that. He said softly, 'Be careful what you wish for. You might get it.'

'W-wish for?' Leo was outraged. 'Are you implying I wish to marry you?'

Amer looked soulful. 'What else is a man to think when a lady pays him the compliment of asking him to marry her?'

Leo choked. 'I did not ask you to marry me.'

'That's what it sounded like to me,' Amer said imperturbably.

Leo stopped feeling even the slightest bit apologetic. She glared.

'I said I'd cut you a deal. That's different.'

He raised his eyebrows. 'I'd be interested to hear how you work that out. Let us have dinner and discuss it.'

'No,' said Leo sharply. 'Thank you,' she added with patent lack of gratitude.

Amer smiled. 'I never sign up to a deal until I have explored the implications.'

She shrugged. 'Fine. So no deal. I can live with that.' She turned away.

He caught her by the arm. Well no, that was not exactly

true. He hardly touched her. But Leo stopped dead as if she had walked into an invisible electric fence.

'And I never turn one down before I've done just that.'

Leo looked over her shoulder at him. Her heart was thundering so hard it was all she could do not to press her hand against her shaken rib cage. What was worse, she was almost certain he knew it. She clenched her hand into a tight, tight fist and kept it at her side.

Amer's remarkable eyes crinkled at the corners as he met hers. The sensuous mouth remained in a prim line but Leo was not deceived. It was an amused, secretive look and it made her blood run cold.

He is laughing at me, she thought.

She said, as haughtily as she knew how, 'My car?'

'Of course.' It was as smooth as cream.

Not taking his hand from her arm he escorted her out into the evening. It had been a hot day and the air was full of the stale heat of combustion engines and too many people. Leo shuddered.

'Sticky,' he agreed with her unspoken distaste. 'You will be glad of a cool drink.'

He must have made some sign, though Leo had not detected it. A long dark car drew up silently in front of them. Amer opened the passenger door.

Leo was not getting caught like that again.

'That's not my car.'

'Of course not.' Amer was shocked. 'When I take a lady out to dinner, I pick her up and see her home.'

'You are not,' said Leo between her teeth, 'taking me out to dinner.'

'I'm glad you feel like that,' Amer said mysteriously.

He shepherded her solicitously into the back seat. To her own fury, Leo found herself complying. He shut the door on her and slipped round to the off side. In the car his smile was very seductive. She recognised that it was designed to be.

'I so much prefer to eat at home.'

Unseduced, Leo narrowed her eyes at all that deceptive openness.

'I'm not cooking for you, either,' she announced.

He chuckled. 'A pleasure deferred.'

'No, it's not. I'm never going to—' Leo broke off, as the car did not turn west as she expected. Instead it slid into Hyde Park and turned right. 'Where are we going?'

Amer widened his eyes at her. 'Why home, of course. Just as you wanted.'

'I live that way,' said Leo, pointing firmly in the direction from which they had come.

He was bland. 'How interesting.'

Leo ground her teeth. 'All right. Whose home?'

'Mine,' he said coolly.

Leo could be cool, too. 'Interesting,' she drawled back at him. 'Would that be the home from home palace or the bachelor pad where anything goes?'

Amer looked amused. 'Which would you prefer?'

Leo resisted the temptation to hit him. Only because she thought it might make her burst into tears. She felt she'd had more fights tonight than she'd had in the whole of her life up to now. She'd not acquitted herself badly. But it had taken more out of her than she could afford if she was going to lock horns with Amer el-Barbary.

She leaned back in her seat with an angry little sigh. A policy of passive resistance, that was the answer. If he got no reaction out of her, Leo reasoned, he would soon get bored and let her go home.

So she managed not to react to the imposing Palladian house. It was no more than she expected after all. She nodded at the butler, managing to stay as impassive as the perfect servant himself. She even kept her cool in the marble entrance hall, though the original Canaletto made her blink a bit. But when Amer led her through the house and out the other side, her strategy tumbled into ruins.

She stopped stock-still, gasping. She was suddenly in the garden of Eden. It was surrounded by an old wall, its stones almost hidden by lush falls of lilac wisteria. Old trees formed a copse at the end of the garden. While a perfect lawn, the grass golden in the late-evening sun, curved away under huge azalea bushes. They were so brilliant with bloom that she could hardly believe it—apricot and lemon and buttercup and champagne; and then a blaze of fiery pink that made her eyes hurt. And the scent! Her senses swam.

'I don't believe it,' Leo whispered.

Amer liked her awe. He smiled.

'Better than the bachelor pad?'

Leo was recalled to herself. She looked at him with dislike.

'It may be beautiful. That doesn't mean that I want to be here.'

'You'd rather we went to the bachelor pad,' he interpreted. He raised a hand. The silent butler materialised.

'Bring the car round.'

The butler inclined his head.

'No,' said Leo hastily. 'No, I don't want to go anywhere else.' In case Amer misunderstood—or pretended to misunderstand—she added with emphasis, 'Until I go home that is.'

Amer bit back a smile.

'Then we will have to drink out here. Unless you are cold?' he added courteously.

Leo was uncomfortably conscious of a heat that had nothing to do with the summer evening.

'No,' she said with constraint.

'Then bring drinks please,' said Amer, every inch the concerned host. 'Dinner in an hour.'

The butler bowed and disappeared.

Leo attempted heavy irony. 'So I'm staying for dinner, am I?'

'I said I would feed you,' Amer reminded her.

'I don't remember accepting.'

He laughed. 'Then do so now.'

And as she looked mulish, he strolled over to her and put

an arm round her shoulders, turning her to face the golden garden.

'Look at that,' he said lazily. 'You can't honestly say you want to leave all this and go back into the dirt of the city.'

For the second time since she had arrived, Leo's senses swam. He was too close. His arm was too heavy. If she turned her head just a fraction, she would rest her cheek against the grey-suited chest. She could smell the warm skin and the faint expensive fragrance of orange flowers and orris.

She remembered that smell. She had thought she would remember it for the rest of her life. Now, she thought with sudden insight, she was going to have to be seriously careful to make sure that was all she remembered from this encounter. The whole evening was turning into an elephant trap for a woman with big feet and minimal experience of seduction.

She gave herself a mental shake and said firmly, 'I can say I don't want to be kidnapped, however.'

For a moment the hand on her upper arm tightened almost unbearably. Not so lazy, now.

'Don't fight me, Leonora.'

She looked up at him indignantly, forgetting for a moment that he was too close.

'Are you threatening me?'

Amer looked down at her. Yes, much too close. The grey eyes were unreadable. But Leo's breath still caught in her throat. Then his lashes dropped and he was lazy again. He gave her shoulders a squeeze, laughing.

'Say thank-you prettily and stop arguing. Let us savour the twilight.'

Leo thought: Something's wrong with me. I want to do what he says. I must be out of my mind.

The butler came back, carrying an enormous embossed tray. He put it on a filigree ironwork table. Still stunned by her unwanted revelation, Leo watched him lift an ornate jug that might have been brass or might—if that were not ridiculous—have been gold. He poured a cloudy liquid into crystal goblets and put them on another tray before presenting them to Amer.

Amer took both and held one out to her. Leo looked at it, not moving. He was amused.

'Lemon, lime, honey and a hint of cinnamon,' he said as if she had voiced her suspicions. 'Maybe a dash of rosewater, though that's a professional secret. Try. If you hate it you can always have more champagne. Though personally, I suspect you're over your limit.'

Leo was so incensed that she grabbed the goblet and swallowed the brew as if it were medicine. She barely tasted it as it went down. She did not care.

'I hate it,' she said deliberately.

Just for a moment the impassive butler was less than impassive. An expression of distinct shock passed over his face, Leo saw. Presumably the Sheikh's usual guests did what he told them and said thank-you for it. Well, this guest was going to be different she thought vengefully.

Amer, of course, was unmoved. 'Then champagne it is.' Without turning his head, he said, 'See to it, Harrods.'

The man left silently.

'Harrods?' said Leo, temporarily diverted. 'Is that really his name?'

'In a way. I dare say you won't approve,' Amer said with wry amusement, 'but the name goes with the job.'

She stared.

'My mother,' he explained. 'When we first bought this house she said the only person she knew in London was the man who delivered her orders from Harrods. Eventually she persuaded him to come and work here. But she had always called him Harrods. So—' He shrugged.

Leo was appalled. 'You made the poor man give up his *name*?'

'I knew you would disapprove,' Amer sighed.

'I think it's barbaric. It's as if you have bought up his whole identity.' She shivered at the thought of such arrogance. 'You really do think you can do anything you want, don't you?'

Amer frowned. 'He could always have left. In fact, he has stayed with us for thirty years.'

But Leo was still chilled by this further evidence of tyranny.

'You set your own rules and everyone else has to obey, don't they?' she said hotly. 'You just think you're above the rest of us.'

Amer was thunderstruck. 'Above— What are you talking about?'

Leo snorted. 'Look at this evening. As I remember, I said I didn't want to have dinner with you several times. Did you take any notice?'

'It's good for you to have new experiences.'

'So you have a right to decide what's good for me now?' raged Leo.

Amer's eyes gleamed.

'More like a duty,' he said blandly.

Leo was utterly unprepared for that.

'What?'

'Well, you keep throwing out challenges.' He gave her his most winning smile. 'What sort of a man would I be if I didn't take them up?'

Leo was speechless.

Harrods returned with a frosted bottle and a crystal flute. Amer flicked his fingers. Harrods surrendered the bottle to him without comment. But as he withdrew Leo thought she detected wintry surprise.

Amer dealt expertly with the bottle and poured the wine. He gave her the glass and took up his own, toasting her.

'Your health.'

Leo was still reeling. She raised her glass but could not think of anything to say. Amer clinked his goblet against hers.

'Truce?'

Looking up, Leo found his eyes were smiling straight into

hers. It made her feel as if the world was suddenly very small and turning so fast that she might fall off. It was all she could do not to grab hold of him to steady herself.

'Come on, Leonora.' It was as smooth as silk and twice as seductive. 'What have you got to lose? Call a truce until sunset.'

She did not trust him an inch.

'What sort of truce?'

His eyes gleamed. 'You don't tear into me and I don't take your hair down.'

Leo choked.

'Truce,' he said firmly and held out his hand.

To her own amazement, Leo found herself giving him her own. This is crazy, she thought. I ought to insist on going home *now*.

But she did not. Instead she let him shake her hand. And then, of course, hold onto it. He ran his fingers over the back of her hand in a movement that was not quite a caress. It set her shivering as none of Simon's most ardent kisses had though.

She hauled her hand back and said the first thing that came into her head.

'Wh-what an interesting garden,' she said quickly. 'No one would think you were in the heart of London.' I sound like my mother, she thought in despair.

Amer frowned.

'Is it difficult to maintain?' gabbled Leo. She held her champagne flute in front of her like an amulet.

Amer's frown deepened. He let out an explosive sigh.

'God spare me from Englishwomen. Every time anyone gets near your feelings you start talking like the Queen.'

Leo decided not to hear that. She started to stroll round the garden, asking intelligent questions about the plants. Their scent was almost overwhelming but she was determined not to let it get to her. Just as she took her wineglass with her but did not drink any more. She needed all her wits about her and she knew it.

So did Amer. He went with her, answering her questions with a barbed politeness that told her he knew exactly what she was doing.

'Bog standard azalea,' he said indifferently as she stopped in front of a ten-foot bush of honey-scented gold.

'H-how interesting.'

He looked down at her ironically. Then a thought occurred to him and his mouth tilted.

'It is, actually. This was the plant that intoxicated Xenophon's soldiers on the way to Trebizond.' He gave her a slow, lazy smile that set her pulses thrumming and her teeth on edge. 'Do you rate your resistance higher or lower?'

Leo's resistance was fraying at the edges with every moment and she suspected he knew it. When he looked at her like that, there did not seem to be much resistance left at all. It was not fair.

He laughed softly. Oh he knew what he was doing all right.

Get a grip, Leo told herself feverishly, *Get a grip.*

'I thought we had a truce?' she managed.

'I haven't laid a hand on you,' he pointed out, all innocence.

She looked at him. He laughed and opened his hands. As if he were letting go of a leading rein, she thought indignantly.

'All right,' he said kindly. 'I won't tease you any more.'

'Thank you.'

'A least not until sunset,' he murmured mischievously.

Leo looked at the sky. It was beginning to darken.

'Perhaps we'd better eat soon.'

'Coward,' he taunted.

But he led the way back to the house and gave the order.

They ate in a small room on the first floor overlooking the garden. Leo hardly knew what the quiet servants put in front of her. She had no appetite and did no more than pick at it.

Amer was concerned.

'Sorry,' said Leo. She was enough her father's daughter to

feel guilty about wasting good food. 'It's been quite a day. I think I just ran out of steam.'

She fully expected him to say something sexy and provocative. But he did not.

Instead he said gravely, 'Because of your broken engagement?'

Leo nursed her left hand. Her ring finger was still slightly sore. She gave a brief, unhappy smile.

'Among other things.'

Amer looked at her thoughtfully.

'Is this where you tell me why you are so anxious to get married?'

Leo jumped. 'I'm not,' she denied hotly.

'That was not the impression you gave me earlier. When you offered me that deal,' he reminded her.

She blushed. 'Yes. Well. I was angry.'

'Evidently.' He paused. 'I am often angry. It has never occurred to me to marry in order to vent my spleen.'

That gave her pause. 'Put like that it doesn't sound very nice.'

'Or very sensible.' He took a peach out of the silver filigree dish and began to peel it casually. Concentrating on the task, he said, 'So answer my question. Why do you—' He corrected himself. 'Why did you think you wanted to marry?'

Leo looked at him. With the steep lids dropped, he was no longer a teasing duellist. Just someone who wanted to know something about her. Not about the business, or her father. Her.

She said abruptly, 'I never thought I'd marry. I've always been the wallflower. I've sort of got used to it. I was going to run the business. I worked hard—' Her voice became suspended.

Amer's brows twitched together in a brief, fierce frown. He must have snicked himself with the knife, she thought.

Not raising his eyes, he said, 'So why Simon Hartley?'

Leo shrugged. 'The Hartleys want to save their stately home. Simon's the eldest son.'

'That explains his side of it,' said Amer without expression. 'What about yours?'

Leo stared out into the garden. Twilight had swathed it in a soft grey that somehow made her want to cry.

'My father doesn't really want me to work in the business, it seems,' she said in a hard voice. 'I needn't have bothered to go to Cairo or anywhere else. He wants to start a dynasty. Work experience isn't much good for that.'

Amer's eyes lifted. He put the peach down and regarded her for a frowning moment.

'And an impoverished aristocrat is?' he drawled.

Leo did not look at him. If she kept her eyes fixed on the garden and very wide, the shaming tears might subside.

'Yes.'

'I see.'

No you don't, she thought. You don't see at all.

She said, 'You must think I'm a fool.'

There was a pause. She did not look at him.

'I think you're a coward,' Amer said coolly.

Leo gasped, her eyes flying to him in spite of herself. He was smiling but the grey eyes were nearly black and there was a pulse throbbing at his temple as if he was so angry he could barely contain himself.

'But not because you did what your father wanted,' he went on. 'I think you did what you wanted. And for all the wrong reasons.' He was not drawling any more.

Leo thought: He sounds furious. He must terrify people when he looks at them like that. Why am I not terrified?

And then her own anger took over.

'How dare you?'

The unamused smile widened. 'You asked,' he clipped.

'You don't know a thing about it.'

Amer was coldly furious.

'I know you didn't get engaged until you realised that I was in the country.'

Leo felt her colour rise. 'What has that got to do with it?' she snapped.

Quite suddenly Amer smiled. 'So you don't deny it.' He sounded pleased with himself.

Damn. She looked away.

'The timing was an unfortunate coincidence,' she said loftily.

He raised his eyebrows.

'It *was.*'

He shrugged. 'Will you tell me something?'

'Probably not,' said Leo, thoroughly disturbed.

'Were you ever in love with him?'

'Simon?' Leo was shocked. 'Of course I—'

He held up a hand. 'Don't lie to me, Leonora. Tell me nothing, if you don't want to. But don't tell me lies.'

Leo was silenced. The fight went out of her all of a sudden. She passed a hand over her eyes.

'I don't know,' she muttered.

'You don't know if you're going to tell me anything? Or you don't know if you loved him?' Amer pressed.

She glared at him. 'Stop interrogating me.'

He laughed. 'All right. Have some peach.' He speared a segment and offered it to her.

She took it. But the little gesture shook Leo. It was too intimate. It seemed to imply that they had eaten like this many times before. And—even more unsettling—would again.

He watched her eat the piece of fruit. His expression was unreadable. So why did she feel as if she had just conceded him a victory?

'I don't understand you,' she burst out.

Amer leaned back in his chair. His body was utterly relaxed. But the sleepy eyes were watchful.

'But I am a simple man.' He was drawling again.

'Huh.'

He laughed. 'I am,' he insisted. 'Simple pleasures. Simple wants.'

Leo surveyed the table eloquently: Venetian crystal, embossed silver, hand-painted china...

'It looks like it,' she said drily.

'Don't judge by appearances,' he chided.

'What else have I got to judge by?'

He considered her thoughtfully.

'You could try asking a few questions.'

'Questions? About what for Heaven's sake?'

Amer raised his eyes to the ceiling. 'Me, you contrary woman,' he said exasperated. 'Don't you want to know anything about me?'

Leo blinked. Was there the faintest undertone of hurt there? Or was it all outraged vanity because she had managed to resist him? After all, he did not know what a struggle she was having to keep to her resolve.

She said drily, 'I know all about you.'

He was pleased. 'You've been asking about me.'

'No, I haven't.'

'Then you don't know anything.'

She gave him her sweetest smile. 'Well, let's just say I know all I need to know. You spelled it out for me.'

He frowned, puzzled. '*I* did?'

Leo said malevolently, '"Come with me to the Casbah", remember?'

His contribution to the Antika Foundation's book! Amer's brow cleared, enlightened.

'Is that what made you sign up with Simon Hartley?' He needed to know for sure.

Leo ground her teeth. 'Will you get rid of the idea that you have any influence on my behaviour? You are nothing to me.'

She thought he would be annoyed. But he was amused. Not just pretending, really amused. Leo looked at him with the deepest suspicion. He laughed aloud.

'Prove it.'

For an outraged second Leo thought she really was going to hit him. She, who had never hit anyone in her life? She clenched her fists in her lap.

'I think it's time I was going,' she said in a suffocated voice.

His eyes danced. 'No coffee?'

'I—'

'Very wise,' he said kindly. 'If you think you can't handle it.'

Leo glared. 'I can handle anything you throw at me,' she announced.

Amer threw back his head and gave another of his deep-throated laughs. She watched, helpless.

'You,' he said when he regained control over his voice, 'are a delight. And a terrible temptation.'

Leo was shaken. No one had ever called her a temptation before. *I knew this dress was too low-cut,* she thought. It was her only coherent thought. The rest was a panicky whirl of half-formed suspicions and wholly impractical escape strategies.

She huddled her shawl round her incendiary décolletage and refused to meet his eyes.

'If I have coffee with you, will you call me a cab?'

'If you still want to go.'

Leo swallowed. 'Then let's have coffee now.'

Having made her bargain, she turned her eyes away dismissively and looked pointedly out of the window.

Amer summoned the butler.

'Coffee in the conservatory,' he told him. With one eye on Leo's averted face, he added in a lower voice, 'And then, I won't be needing you again tonight.'

It was not the first time the butler had received such instructions from Amer. His expression did not change.

'Certainly, Your Excellency. And do you wish to speak to Mr Farah?'

'No,' said Amer unequivocally. He stood up and held out a hand to Leo.

'Come and see some more plants you can interrogate me about.'

Ignoring the hand, she got up and followed him. I must

not bump into the furniture, she thought hazily. I could not bear it if I blundered into one of his priceless bits of art in my dash for the door. With today's luck, I'd probably break it.

The conservatory ran the entire length of the house and looked out onto the now twilit garden. Discreetly placed lights illuminated palms, vines and a column of jasmine, covered with fragrant star flowers. At one end a wall-mounted fountain played. Leo's lips parted in amazement.

'Yes, you like that, don't you?' Amer was wry. 'I'm beginning to think botany is the only thing that turns you on.'

Leo swung round indignantly—and bumped into the butler, bearing the coffee tray silently behind her.

The butler recovered his balance. Not so the tray he was carrying. China flew, and the coffeepot tipped its contents in a neat stream down the front of her dress.

Leo closed her eyes. 'Today's luck strikes again.'

Amer whisked the stained shawl away from her. 'See what can be done with that Harrods.'

The butler bore it off rapidly.

Amer was blotting the hot coffee with an impeccable white handkerchief. His hands were quite impersonal. Leo swallowed and opened her eyes hurriedly. She was disconcerted to find that she did not feel impersonal at all.

He stood back, dissatisfied. 'This is soaked. We'll have to do better than this.' A thought occurred to him. 'Come with me.'

He whisked her up two flights of stairs to an imposing set of double doors in shining mahogany. Leo was taken aback. But Amer flung open their magnificence as casually as if they led to a broom cupboard and ushered Leo inside.

It was not a broom cupboard, of course. It was a bedroom. The most sumptuous bedroom she had ever seen. Luxury like this was something that Leo, well-off and widely travelled though she was, had never even imagined.

Gulping, Leo looked round in disbelief. It was like a renaissance prince's salon. The room she was standing in was enormous. Carved pillars supported a domed ceiling that was clearly intended to represent the sky and was nearly as big. The wooden floor had been polished until it shone like wine. Great swathes of gold brocade framed tall windows. One entire wall was painted with a desert hunting scene. Against it stood a gilded couch upholstered in royal blue and scattered with gold cushions.

And the bed. Leo swallowed hard. She kept an eye on that bed. It looked dangerous. It was big and low and *rich;* ebony inlaid with intricate gold decoration; and it was covered with a shimmering cloth that she had very little doubt was woven gold.

She said the first thing that came into her head.

'*Simple* pleasures, my eye.'

Amer was shaken by a silent laugh. 'Design approved by my cousin the Minister for Culture, I'm sorry you don't approve of his taste.' He waved a hand at the couch. 'Take off that wet dress and sit down. I'll find you something to wear.'

He disappeared through a door behind a pillar.

Leo unzipped her dress and sank down onto the couch, holding the damp cloth modestly in front of her. A tubular cushion fell squashily to the floor, its ornate tassels flying wide. Gold thread unravelled. It pooled on the polished floor like tangled knitting.

She winced. Leo Groom, true to form, causing devastation wherever she set her clumsy feet. It was the last straw. Leo choked and began to cry.

Amer appeared at once, a robe of some sort over his arm.

'What's the matter?' he said, concerned.

Leo looked up. 'I've spoiled your cushion,' she said tragically.

She pointed at the puddle of gold braiding on the floor. It had hooked itself round the diamanté motif on her smart black shoe and before she got it off became ten times more tangled than before.

Amer was blank. He cast the robe from him and went down on one knee beside her. Very gently he put a fingertip to her eye. Sure enough, when he removed it there was a tear on the end of it.

'You cry over a *cushion?*' he said in disbelief.

'I always spoil things,' said Leo. She sniffed. 'I always have. I'm clumsy. I break things and fall over things and get coffee down my dress...' Her voice became suspended.

'I count your getting coffee on your dress as a bonus,' he said softly. 'Believe me.'

Leo turned drowned brown eyes to his. He smoothed the anxiety lines from her forehead with a gentle finger.

'Believe me,' he repeated, his voice suddenly husky.

With a little gesture of surrender Leo leaned forward and rested her head against his chest.

'I think this has been the worst day of my life,' she said, her voice muffled in the ivory silk of his shirt.

Amer stroked her hair. His hand was not entirely steady. Leo was unaware of it.

'No, it hasn't,' he said caressingly. 'You broke off an engagement you should never have got into. And you put me in my place. Can't be all bad.'

Leo gave a choke of startled laughter.

'Put you in your place?' she echoed drily. 'Oh sure.'

She looked up and met his eyes. They were warm, the grey of the soft twilight sky outside. Intent. And very close indeed.

Leo drew a shaky breath. There was that fugitive cologne again. Leo moistened her lips. The scent of it seemed to curl round her like smoke, like fog, awaking all her senses.

She said uncertainly, 'I—'

Suddenly it did not seem to matter that she was an emotional mess; or clumsy; or not wanted in the business. She was in his arms—well, almost in his arms—and it was Heaven.

Amer touched her cheek. 'Hush,' he said. 'Hush.'

This time she did notice that he was shaking. It was a gentle gesture. No force. No demand. It should have been kind and comforting, but the tremor in his fingers distracted her and it was neither.

For a long moment they looked at each other in silence. Leo thought hazily: I've been here before. This is how he made me feel that night. I want...I *want*...

Very, very gently, he prised the dress out of her unresisting fingers. Her lace-covered breasts started at the sudden chill. She heard him catch his breath.

'Beautiful,' he said reverently.

Leo turned her head away. Acute need warred with acute embarrassment. She vibrated with tension.

Taking his time, Amer stroked the lace aside and bent his head. Leo kept her head turned away. She held her breath. Very softly he brushed his lips across the nipple he had uncovered. She groaned.

'Truce over, I think,' he murmured. 'Don't you?'

Leo was beyond answering; beyond concentrating on anything but this incredible feeling.

'Time we were somewhere more comfortable.'

He was on his feet. Leo watched him, dazed. He twitched the corner of the gold coverlet. It rippled off the bed like a water snake.

'Scratchy,' explained Amer.

He slid his arms round her, lifting. She could feel his every tiny muscle movement in her fingers' ends.

He laid her down so gently. She hardly felt her silks and laces slide away until he replaced them with the warm sensuousness of his mouth. Leo could not believe it. He ran his open palm possessively over her naked hip and she shivered. Nothing had ever prepared her for this exquisite sensitivity. It was so piercing that it was almost like pain. But at the same time it was like being bathed in sunlight. She closed her eyes, drifting in delight.

'I'm glad you grew your hair.' It was a whisper.

Leo turned her head to look at him. He was drawing the pins out of her sophisticated hairstyle and fanning her hair out on his pillow. He ran his hands through it, watching absorbedly.

'I knew I would do this,' he murmured.

He shifted his gaze and smiled down at her, right into her eyes. Wonderingly she put up a hand to touch his mouth, his cheekbones, the corner of those silver eyes.

He stilled. For a moment his eyes were not silver any more, or gentle. And all vestige of amusement left his face. For a moment he looked as if he was in agony.

Leo was alarmed. 'What is it?'

But he did not answer. Or not with words. Instead he bent over her unhurriedly and his hands began to move. They smoothed and moulded and explored every inch of her body. Slowly. Then his mouth followed the same path down her pliant limbs with butterfly kisses.

Leo had never imagined such exquisite sensations. Soon she was writhing with pleasure and a wholly new hunger. Eyes tight shut, she reached for him.

He let her get rid of his jacket, even helped her with the buttons of his shirt so that she could feel the amazing sensation of her cool, quivering flesh against his warmth. But that was as far as he permitted.

'No,' he said, catching her clumsy, seeking hands.

Leo froze and her eyes flew open.

Amer saw her reaction. His eyes darkened. Suddenly he was unhurried no longer. He pushed her back, his mouth urgent at her breast, his hands shifting her as if he knew without words what her body required. His fingers circled, spiralled, drew her irresistibly into a dark vortex of response.

Leo cried out. Amer said something harsh she did not hear—or did not understand—and then his caress deepened urgently.

A rhythm she did not know she knew took hold of Leo. She arched and arched. Her heart raced. The strange, fierce sensation made her cry out, almost in fear.

Just for a moment she saw Amer's expression. It was total triumph.

And then she convulsed and the world spun out of control.

CHAPTER SEVEN

IT WAS Amer who stirred first. Leo was lying across his chest, breathing in the scent of him. She felt shattered by her own sensations. At the same time the dark pulse still throbbed, cavernously deep, waiting to reignite, waiting to meet its fellow.

Now, she thought. Now he will get rid of his clothes. Now he will lose himself, too. This time we will travel together.

She could hardly breathe as he fanned her hair about her bare shoulders.

It feels like silk, she thought. It amazed and delighted her. *My* hair feels like silk. What has he done to me? She turned her head, and quickly, shyly, kissed the warm golden chest where his heart beat so steadily.

But he did not respond. And he did not kiss her again.

He said, 'You'll get cold.'

'Mmm?'

He caressed the curve of her shoulder as if he owned it. As if he savoured the ownership. But not with passion.

'I can't have you catching cold.' His voice was full of lazy laughter. 'Think what it would do for my reputation.'

Leo's heart turned over. Hardly believing it, she thought: He has had enough of me already.

She was shaken to the core by the sensations of the last few minutes. She had never even imagined feelings like that existed, far less that she was capable of them. And now she lay in his arms, getting colder and colder, tasting rejection as she had never imagined that, either.

But she had started the evening fighting back and she was not going to fall into a decline now. With a courage she did

115

not know she possessed, Leo raised her head and narrowed her eyes at him.

'For that matter, what would it do for your reputation to have it known that you seduce women by pouring coffee all over them?' she taunted.

'Would you call it seduction?' he murmured.

Leo winced inwardly. But she continued as if she had not heard. 'The least I was expecting was candlelight and a string quartet to serenade me.'

Amer looked at her curiously. 'I'll do better next time,' he promised.

He picked up her hand and carried it to his mouth. In spite of herself, Leo could feel her muscles uncurl in response. Her eyes grew slumberous. Amer smiled and turned her hand over so he could press a kiss into the palm. Every nerve ending in Leo quivered.

Surely now he would...

But he was swinging off the bed, refastening his shirt.

'Come along, my little sensualist. I'll give you candlelight and your serenade if you let me wrap you up in something warm first.'

He dropped a soft velour robe over her. It was the colour of tawny port and sported the inevitable gold facings. She huddled into it, grateful for not having to pretend any more that she did not mind him looking at her nakedness.

Something in her expression must have given her away. Amer's brows twitched together.

Quickly she flipped the gold braid with a disparaging finger. 'More design courtesy of the Minister of Culture?'

'Probably.'

Amer sat on the edge of the bed beside her. He put his hand against her cheek, savouring the warmth.

'I've never seen such skin.' He pulled the velour aside and kissed her shoulder. 'Pale as moonlight. We have poems about that, you know. Up to now I thought it was a poetic invention.'

He pulled her against his shoulder. At once, of course, he felt the rigidity in her body.

'What is it?' he said concerned.

She could not bear any more. Scrambling off the bed she dived for the bathroom door. She banged it behind her and leaned against it, letting the tears fall at last.

It was only a brief storm. She was careful to make no sound. And when it was over, she bathed her eyes and flushed face. To steady herself, she took stock of the bathroom.

It was on the same excessive lines as the master bedroom. It had marble floors and Greek columns. And a round sunken bath that was clearly designed for more than one person. Arched niches following the curved wall held statues and urns as well as a startling selection of expensive oils. Even the soap was sculptured.

Leo picked up a creamy bar and sniffed experimentally. There was a shadow on the pale bar. She rubbed at it and realised that it was ink transferred from her own finger.

'Leonora Groom, walking disaster,' she muttered. 'You may go to bed with princes but you still have the writing habits of a fourth former. How many times have you washed your hands since you acquired that stain? Ten? Fifteen? It must be ground in.'

She put the soap down hurriedly and a faint elusive scent wafted up to her. Amer's! She would know it anywhere. She backed away from the bath as if he were lying in it, laughing at her.

'Time to go back to walking disaster mode,' she told herself.

She went back into the bedroom and announced, 'I've got to go,' before her resolve wore off.

Amer was standing at the window, looking down into the garden. Just for a moment as he turned his head, she thought he looked strained. But at her words he raised his eyebrows in surprise.

'Run that past me again.'

The look of surprise was almost Leo's undoing.

Remember his own words, she told herself. He had been quite specific in that little piece of satire. Any opportunity for seduction should be pursued. With any woman. She had handed him the opportunity on a plate and he had not even bothered to seduce her. Would it have been better if he had?

Leo swallowed. 'I've got to go.'

She scrabbled for her clothes.

'Hey.'

He skirted the great tumbled bed and strolled over to her, stopping her search by the simple expedient of putting one hand round her wrist and holding it. In spite of herself, Leo shivered with lust. How could he do that, just by touching her arm? When he didn't even want her. It was *cruel*.

'What's the matter?'

He was smiling. He didn't think it was serious. Well, of course, for him it wasn't serious.

Or for her, either, Leo told herself feverishly. It was all over emotional nonsense at the end of a highly charged day. She would see that in the morning.

As long as she was alone in the morning, of course.

'I must get home. Things to do. Work,' said Leo.

The excuses floundered but the desperation was evident. Amer let go of her wrist and stood back, frowning.

'I thought we would spend the evening together.'

He encountered a look of such horror from Leo that he blinked.

'Evidently not,' he answered himself drily.

'I'm sorry,' said Leo, in disarray.

She grabbed her clothes and dived back into the bathroom. She was crying again.

She scrambled rapidly back into her dress. There was nothing she could do about her hair or—she winced at her reflection—the softly swollen mouth. There was no disguising the fact that she looked like a woman who had made love. At least she did until you got to her eyes.

They looked like a woman who had walked into a nightmare and could not find her way back.

Leo looked away. She tidied her dress, trying to reduce its plunge without much success.

'I am never,' she promised herself, 'going to wear this dress again.'

She ran her hands through the tangle of hair, trying not to remember how it had felt running through Amer's fingers. She could not put it up again—she had no idea what had happened to her hairpins and she was not going to go rummaging among tumbled bedclothes to find out—but at least she could make it lie flat to her head.

She thrust her feet into the sophisticated shoes and felt a measure of normality return. She picked up his robe, straightened her shoulders and went back to face Amer.

He had no smile for her.

'Are you all right?'

'Of course,' said Leo, not looking at him.

He put an arm round her shoulders. Just for a moment she felt protected. It was heavenly.

It was also an illusion. She twitched away from him and bolted for the stairs. Amer let her go without comment. But his frown deepened as he went after her.

Leo dived back to the salon where they had supper. The garden beyond the window was now completely dark. Someone had turned on the lights but they were dim and atmospheric. Breathy saxophone music whispered from hidden speakers. There was another tray of coffee—this time with a vacuum coffeepot—on the table.

Leo stopped dead in the doorway.

'A real Don Juan's box of tricks,' she said bitterly.

At her shoulder, Amer stopped, a look of comprehension flashing across his face. For a moment he was disturbed. Then he took a decision.

'Don Juan?' he murmured, ushering her into the room. 'Unfair. Have you forgotten we're going to be married?'

Leo recoiled as if she had burned herself.

'Nonsense.'

'Well, you asked me,' he reminded her evenly. 'Have some coffee and let's discuss it.'

She looked at him with hot eyes. 'There's nothing to discuss. And I don't want any coffee. I want to go home. Will you call me a cab?'

Amer was shocked. 'Of course not.'

Leo glared. 'You mean I'll have to make a break for it and pick one up in the street?'

He was silent for a moment. Then he said, 'Leonora, what's wrong?'

She shook her head, blinking away tears.

'Did I rush you? I thought if—'

But she stopped him with a gesture so despairing that he could not push her. He sighed.

'If you insist on going I will drive you. Of course. Only—' he gave her his most winning smile '—I hope you'll stay.'

The smile did not work. It was almost as if she did not see it. As if she would not allow herself to see it.

To Amer's deep disquiet, he found himself driving through the electronic gates of the Wimbledon mansion forty minutes later.

'Yours?' he said, genuinely disconcerted by the mansion confronting him.

Leo gave a sharp laugh. 'My father's. I have the extension.'

'Ah.'

It was no more than a sound but Leo detected patronising, even criticism.

'What?' she said, bristling. 'What?'

Amer did not answer. Or not directly.

'Are you allowed to ask me in?'

'It's quite self-contained,' Leo retorted. 'We don't police each other.'

He was noncommittal. 'Really.'

'Come in, if you don't believe me,' said Leo goaded.

He did not need a second invitation.

She switched on all the lights defiantly. No seducer's shadowy atmospherics here. He looked round, interested. Leo had not realised how untidy her sitting room was before. The desk, computer and television were islands among the flotsam—magazines, newspapers, open books, unanswered letters, theatre programmes, the dry cleaning she had dumped on the sofa two days ago...

'I see you live alone,' said Amer with quiet satisfaction.

'You knew that.'

'I thought Simon Hartley might have acquired residency rights.'

'No,' said Leo shortly.

'So I see.' He sounded inordinately pleased about it. 'What are you going to do about him?'

Back on her home territory Leo was feeling braver. She was also feeling appalled at her own conduct this evening.

'It's already done. Not that it's any of your business.'

'Of course it is. I can't have another man thinking he's engaged to my fiancé.'

She found she could not parry his teasing any more. She felt deathly tired suddenly.

'Oh go away,' said Leo, at the end of her tether.

'All right,' Amer said peacefully. He touched her cheek briefly. 'But don't forget you asked me to marry you.'

Leo ground her teeth. 'I'm not likely to forget that piece of insanity.'

'And I accepted.'

'Don't talk nonsense.'

His eyes sparkled but he shook his head reproachfully. 'You can't get out of it that way. You're mine now.'

'Get out,' Leo yelled.

He smiled deep into her eyes, kissed the air between them and went.

Leo did not sleep well. Well, that was not for the first time and, in the circumstances, not surprising. She had even expected it. What she had not expected was that work would not be the all-engrossing antidote that it usually was. Twice she found her concentration drifting away from the papers in front of her. And once she forgot a meeting altogether and had to be smuggled in late. The only time she came fully into the present was when her secretary buzzed to say that Mr el-Barbary was on the phone for her.

'I'm not taking his calls,' snapped Leo.

By the end of the day Leo's temper was on a hair trigger and her secretary was torn between panic and tears. When Gordon Groom stormed into the office, it was the last straw. He only ever came out of the Chief Executive's suite when there was a crisis but, Joanne thought she had never seen him in a rage like this.

'What the hell do you think you're playing at?' he shouted, steaming straight into Leo's room without even checking whether she was alone.

'Hello, Pops,' said Leo. 'You got back from Singapore quickly. Did Simon call for backup?'

She twirled her executive chair round a couple of times and grinned brazenly. 'I'm free.'

Gordon was white with temper. 'Simon rang me and I came at once. What is this nonsense all about?'

'I'm sure Simon told you. We decided to break our engagement.'

'But you've only just got the bloody ring.'

'That,' agreed Leo gravely, 'is true.'

'It's no laughing matter.' Gordon was furious.

Leo tilted her head on one side thoughtfully.

'Oh I don't know. I got away without ruining my life. That must be worth a mild titter. I could have married a man who thought it was part of his job description.'

Her father's face darkened. 'That's not funny.'

'I don't think so, either.' She stood up. Suddenly she let her own fury run out on its leash. It was a heady feeling. 'In fact I think the whole thing with Simon was seriously un-funny. And all because I let myself be manipulated by the two of you.'

He gobbled.

'Don't get me wrong,' said Leo in a light, hard voice. 'I don't blame you. I blame myself. I should have had the guts to make my own choices. From now on I'm going to.'

Gordon realised that, for the first time since she was a small child, he was probably not going to get his Leo to do what he wanted. Shock and affront made him lose what little command over himself he had left.

'You needn't think you can stay on here as my pensioner,' he raged. 'If you want to make your own choices, fine. And pay your own bills while you're at it.'

In the act of pushing back her chair, Leo stopped dead. She stared at him, breathing hard.

'Your *pensioner?*'

'You don't think you earn the damned great salary I pay you, do you?' said Gordon cruelly.

She was suddenly very pale.

'No,' she said very quietly. 'Any more than I earned the right to live in the Wimbledon house. I take it this is a notice to quit?'

'Oh for God's sake.' Gordon was scathing. 'Spare me the melodrama.' He strove for control. 'Look, can't we sit down and discuss this rationally?'

'There's nothing to discuss, Father.' Her voice was almost inaudible but quite composed. 'When it come to my marriage you don't get a vote.'

'Then—'

She flung up a hand. 'No more threats, please.'

To tell the truth, Gordon was shaken by what he seemed to have done. Leo had never turned on him like that before. He was temperamentally incapable of backing down but he did realise he had gone too far.

'We've both said things we'll be sorry for,' he said heavily. 'Grooms is the only future you've got, one way or another. Go home and think about it. We'll talk in the morning.'

Leo did not answer him. He gave an exasperated exclamation and stalked out.

She sank back into her chair, shaking.

What am I going to do, Leo thought. What in the wide world am I going to do?

It did not take long for Amer to deduce that Leo was not talking to him. No one could be *that* busy. He frowned. In spite of what she had said last night, in spite of his own careful strategy, he was not entirely surprised.

He looked unseeingly at the file that Major McDonald had left. What went wrong last night? He had thought he'd done well, in the circumstances.

He had seen at once that it was more than the champagne that had sent Leo into that raging temper. But the champagne had fired a recklessness which he did not need his investigator's report to tell him was out of character. And he had so nearly taken advantage of it.

'I should have done. Then she would really have a reason for not taking my calls,' Amer said savagely.

He did not quite know why he had not. He was not used to denying himself. And God knows she had been alluring, in her wide-eyed amazement at how he made her feel.

And yet… And yet…

There had been something heartbreakingly unguarded about her last night. When she touched his face she seemed so young; as if she had found herself in wonderland and could not believe what she was doing here.

Quite suddenly he had wanted to keep that look of wonder on her face. To give, for once, without taking. It had seemed like a way of taking care of her.

Now he shifted uneasily. He was not used to that protective urge, either. It was disconcerting. Oh yes, he had been right when he told Hari he would go to any lengths to make her listen to him. Though he had not realised himself then, quite how much he meant it.

He opened the file again. The notice of her engagement stared out at him. Amer frowned, furious again.

And then—he read it again. "Daughter of blah, blah and Mrs Deborah Groom of Kensington." Unless he was much mistaken he had already met Mrs Deborah Groom of Kensington. And she had lied to him, too. So she owed him, didn't she?

He reached for a telephone directory.

The first thing, Leo knew, was to get out of her father's house. Even though the flat was theoretically self-contained, Gordon Groom still thought of it as his territory.

She rang her mother.

'Darling,' said Deborah. 'How lovely. Do you want to get together and talk weddings?'

Leo laughed so hard that she could barely speak. When she controlled herself enough to explain, her mother was un-usually silent.

'So what are you going to do?'

'I thought I might come and stay?' Leo said tentatively.

Deborah was brisk. 'Out of the question. I'm off to Spain and the flat is being completely remodelled while I'm away. No power, no water. Uninhabitable. Sorry darling.'

But she did not, thought Leo shrewdly, sound sorry.

'Well, I could always stay with Claire...'

'When you're running away from her brother?' Deborah gave a shriek of shocked laughter. 'Leo, you're the *end*.'

'But—'

'What you need,' said her mother sapiently, 'is a nice for-eign holiday. Get yourself a tan and let your hair down a bit. You'll come back a new woman.'

Leo knew it was exactly what her mother would do in similar circumstances. For the first time since Gordon had marched into her room, she smiled, albeit faintly.

'Thanks. But I'm not sure it would work for me.'

'Works for everyone, darling,' Deborah assured her

blithely. 'Especially if you can find a nice man to help you have fun.'

Unbidden, unwelcome, the thought of Amer, his face contorted with triumph, flashed across Leo's inner eye. She shuddered.

'I've had all the men I can handle in the last week,' she said unwarily.

Deborah chuckled. 'Oh well, there's your answer,' she said pleased. 'Have fun, darling.' She rang off.

Amer did not make the mistake of telephoning again. He established Leo's movements by means of various devious and highly expensive means. What he learned, caused him to suck his teeth and make a number of international phone calls.

And then he plotted his strategy.

Leo was throwing things into suitcases when the bell rang. For a moment she thought it was her father and almost did not answer. But a quick look at her watch reassured her. Even for a major domestic crisis, Gordon Groom would not be home before seven.

So she smoothed her hands down the side of her dusty jeans and went to open the door. For a moment she did not recognise the tall, casually dressed man in dark glasses.

'You're home early,' said Amer displeased.

He did not wait to be invited but, taking off his dark glasses, walked past her into the sitting room. At the sight that met his eyes, he halted, his brows rising at the chaos.

'I thought it could not get more untidy than when I first saw it,' he remarked. 'I see I was wrong.'

Leo was in no mood to provide the cabaret.

'Packing,' she said shortly. 'I'm moving out.'

He nodded approvingly. 'I'm flattered you took my words to heart.'

Leo was speechless.

'Living in your father's pocket,' he explained kindly. 'Not healthy. Believe me, I speak from experience.'

Leo did not want to hear about his experience. She said so.

Amer beamed, not a whit offended. 'I hear you've made it a clean break all round. Excellent.'

Leo was not given to self-pity. She would have said the last thing she wanted was sympathy from Amer or anyone else. But somehow this cheery acceptance that losing her home and her job in one day was somehow life enhancing was too much to bear. For a wild moment she nearly launched herself at him, screaming.

But one look at the gleam in his eyes made her realise that this was exactly what he hoped for. She drew on all her reserves of self-control and kept quiet. Still, she retired behind a small coffee table in case the temptation to hit him became too great to resist.

'How did you know that?' she said acidly. 'Have you been spying on me again?'

Amer smiled. This was clearly a question he had anticipated.

'Interested enquiries into your welfare,' he said smoothly. 'I wondered if your father would give you grief after your bid for freedom.'

Leo winced. 'Shrewd of you.'

He laughed but his expression was sympathetic. 'When it comes to overbearing fathers, mine wrote the book,' he said wryly. 'Listen to the voice of experience. What you need now is a cooling off period.'

'Why do you think I'm packing?' snapped Leo.

'Got anywhere to go?'

She hesitated.

'I thought not. That's why I'm here.'

Leo regarded him with deep suspicion. 'I don't understand.'

Amer offered her a blinding smile. 'I'm offering you sanctuary.'

Leo's suspicions crystallised. Her temper, simmering all day, seemed to shoot out of the top of her head.

'How dare you?' she yelled.

Amer blinked.

'I'm not moving in with you. Not if you were the last man on earth. And if you think a disaster in my private life will push me into your arms, you've got me very wrong.'

There was a very nasty silence. Amer had not moved. But all of a sudden he looked dangerous.

'You are insulting,' he said softly.

Leo quailed inwardly. But she was not going to admit it.

'And you're an opportunist,' she flung back at him.

'You are so wrong,' he said. 'Was I an opportunist last night?'

Leo paled.

'Let me assure you—' his voice was very soft but the grey eyes were like chips of flint '—you have no need to fear me. I have never wanted you less than I do at this moment.'

'*Oh.*' Leo was so angry that she was not even upset. Maybe later, she thought. Now she just wanted to hit him. 'How dare you?'

'The last thing any man wants is a woman who thinks she has no alternative,' Amer told her. His voice bit. 'What fun is there in a woman who has been pushed into your arms?'

'In that case—'

He swept on, ignoring her. 'A man,' he said very softly, 'does his own hunting.'

Leo felt the shock go through her as if she had walked into a block of ice. For a moment it left her quite numb. Her brain was working. But nothing else.

She shook her head. 'I don't believe you said that.'

'Believe it.'

Her body came back on line. She found it was shaking. Was she afraid of him? The idea was insupportable.

'I don't like threats,' she hissed.

'What threats?'

'You implied I was some sort of—prey.' Leo could not help herself. She shuddered.

'That's nonsense and you know it. Prey gets killed. That's not what I want to do to you at all.'

She was not going to ask him what he did want to do to her. She was *not*.

'And you know that, too. You ought to.' The caressing note was back. Was it calculated? She just did not know. All she knew was that it was too horribly reminiscent of last night.

Reluctant, ashamed, Leo met his eyes. She could see that he was remembering last night, too. And she had almost managed to blank it out of her memory. Yet suddenly it was there in the room with them: what she had said. What, Heaven help her, she had done.

Leo shut her eyes. 'Please go.'

'No,' said Amer unhelpfully. 'You're my promised wife. I have a responsibility.'

Leo opened her eyes and glared. 'Will you please,' she said intensely, 'stop calling me your promised wife You know perfectly well I didn't mean it.'

'But I did.'

She could have danced with rage. 'Well too bad. Because I'm not going to marry anybody, And—'

There was a long peal on the doorbell.

'Now what?' said Leo exasperated.

She trod round the coffee table and suitcases and went to answer it. To her amazement it was her father.

'Pops!'

'May I come in?'

Leo was blank. Gordon Groom never came to her bit of the house. If he wanted to see her he left a message at work. A couple of times he had called and asked her over to the main house on the spur of the moment. But turn up humbly on her doorstep like any ordinary visitor? Never. She could not believe it.

'Yes, if you—' She remembered Amer. 'Well—'

Gordon did not notice her reluctance. He shouldered past her, frowning with his own preoccupations.

'You were worked up earlier,' he said. 'Now you've had time to think rationally—'

He caught sight of Amer. At once his hackles rose. Leo saw it with a sinking heart.

'This isn't a good time, Pops,' she began. Her voice shook.

Gordon did not take any notice of her. He thrust his chin out pugnaciously.

'Who are you?' he demanded.

Amer looked at Leo. She seemed frozen. Gordon swung back on her.

'How long has he been here? Have you been seeing someone behind Simon's back? Is that why Simon dumped you?'

Leo said numbly, 'Simon didn't dump me.'

Gordon ignored that, too. He gave a crow of triumph. 'I knew there had to be more in it that you said. I just knew it. You *fool*.'

It was like all their other arguments, ever since she was a child. The loud, hectoring voice, the refusal to listen to her— Leo knew it so well. And she still did not know how to deal with it.

'I'll call him,' said Gordon, the fixer, pursuing his own train of thought. 'See if I can smooth things over. He's a good lad. He'll listen to reason.'

Leo could feel the familiar helplessness swelling up until it closed her throat. She felt suffocated.

She found an arm round her shoulders.

'You are right,' Amer said quietly. 'I am Leonora's lover.'

Leo flinched. Then, under the pressure of his fingers, stood perfectly still. She felt numb.

Gordon was diverted briefly from his plotting. He looked impatient.

'Not any more you're not.'

It was his turn to be ignored.

'And I am going to marry her.'

CHAPTER EIGHT

TWELVE hours later Leo was on a plane.

Amer, more businesslike than she had ever seen him, had simply taken charge. She had been swept off to spend the night in a quietly exclusive hotel. And then this morning Hari Farah had arrived with her passport, tickets and instructions to accompany her to Dalmun.

Leo had not slept and she was feeling spaced out. Although Hari was exquisitely polite she regarded him with suspicion.

'Where is Amer?'

'He has some matters to arrange. Nothing of significance. But long-standing arrangements will need to be changed,' said Hari smoothly, conveniently forgetting the acrimonious telephone call that had been in progress when he left the Mayfair house. The old Sheikh had not been at all pleased at his son's news and was saying so at length.

Leo was too proud to ask any more. Anyway, there was no point in asking Hari the most burning question in her mind.

Why had Amer left her alone last night? She would have resisted to the point of violence if Amer had assumed that because he had decided for some reason of his own that it amused him to rescue her from her predicament, he was entitled to make love to her, of course. But she was disconcerted that he had not even tried.

So she allowed herself to be swept off to the airport, still in a daze from her sleepless night. Amer had managed a brief, courteous phone call this morning. But that was all.

'What is he *doing?*' she said to herself as much as Hari.

Hari did not answer. He was too polite. He could have

131

said he wished he knew. In all the years he had known him he had never seen Amer like this.

He had even said so, during the dawn telephone calls.

'Why are you doing this?'

'I'm going to marry her,' Amer replied.

Hari was grim. 'Since when?'

'Since she asked me.'

'Since she—' Hari was lost for words.

'Well, to be honest since she dared me not to.'

'You're crazy,' said Hari finding words came to mind after all. 'And what's more so is she.'

'Oh no, she's got very cold feet now.'

'Cold feet? You mean she wants to back out and you won't let her?'

'That's not a very romantic way of putting it,' said Amer reproachfully.

'Romantic! You *are* crazy.' A thought occurred to Hari. 'You're not in love with her, are you?'

Amer hesitated. 'She asked me to marry her,' he said obstinately. 'She's not going to wriggle out of it.'

'She'll hate you,' said Hari with gloomy satisfaction.

'But she'll learn not to go asking men to marry her because she's lost her temper.'

Hari stared at Amer. 'You're not serious.'

Amer stared back, implacable.

'You *are* serious. You can't do this. Not just to teach the girl a lesson.'

'I can do whatever I want,' Amer said haughtily.

Hari despaired and said so. Amer was unmoved. Hari banged off to pack.

When he had gone, Amer's arrogant smile died. He was not going to admit it to Hari but he knew that what he was doing was irrational.

At first she had just infuriated him, throwing out her challenging proposal like that as if he were negligible, a *nothing* in her life. He had needed, really needed, as he told her last night, to show her he was a man who did his own hunting. And made sure that every one else knew that she was *his* and no one else's. Hell, he had even been jealous of her dictatorial old father.

But there was more to it than that. He wanted to treasure her, to make her feel safe; to make her feel *wonderful*. To make her look again as she had in his arms, bewildered by bliss. And he wanted it forever.

And if she didn't want it, too bad! He straightened his shoulders. She would in time. If it was the last thing he did, he would make her want him as he wanted her.

Leo, in Hari's charge after Amer's polite and passionless phone call, had given up thinking. She told herself she did not want passion from Amer. Of course she did not. But the lack of it made her feel lost and even more bereft than her departure from home and job.

She hid it, allowing Hari to usher her into the first-class cabin and to probe—discreetly—into her relationship with his boss. Since she did not know what it all meant herself she did not give much for his chances of enlightenment.

'I am just coming to Dalmun for a visit,' Leo announced. 'My mother thinks I need a holiday somewhere warm.'

She said it several times. It sounded increasingly hollow. Hari, however, was too polite to say so.

She was clearly exhausted. He let her snooze. Time enough to pass on some essential background information when she was more alert.

She woke when the cabin crew started to serve lunch.

'I took the liberty of ordering for you,' Hari told her. 'You were sleeping so peacefully. But if you do not like anything, they will be only too happy to fetch you something else.'

'I'm sure it will be fine,' muttered Leo.

Awake at last, she wondered what on earth she was getting herself into. What she doing on this plane? How could she have let Amer el-Barbary take charge of her life like that? If she needed an exotic holiday why had she not gone to the Seychelles or Barbados on her own?

Because, said a cynical little voice inside her, nobody goes to the Seychelles or Barbados on their own. And Amer el-Barbary had not stopped to ask her permission.

'I am sure you will find it interesting,' Hari said diplomatically. 'Er, what exactly has His Excellency told you about the country?'

His Excellency! Leo winced. Hari could not have said anything which made her realise how far away her world was from Amer's. Or how little she knew about him really.

'Nothing very much at all,' she muttered.

Hari hid his dismay and embarked on a rapid thumbnail sketch.

'It is very old. Dalmun City was on the frankincense road.'

Leo struggled to concentrate. It felt as if she were in the middle of a nightmare.

'The frankincense road?'

'It went along the edge of the desert,' Hari explained. 'In the monsoon season, traders sailed to India and even China. They brought back all sorts of things that people wanted in Europe. Silks, feathers, spices. The road developed to take exotic goods north to the markets.'

Silks, feathers and spices. Exotic indeed. And for all Amer's Italian suits and Impressionist paintings, that was his real heritage. And she knew nothing of it at all.

Just because he could set her senses on fire, it did not mean that they had anything like enough to bridge that centuries-deep gap of culture. Leo felt very cold.

Hari ploughed on conscientiously. 'At one time there were several cities strung out along the road where the merchants would stop and trade. Just ruins now, of course. That is where His Excellency got his interest in archaeology, of course.'

'Amer is interested in archaeology? I didn't know,' said Leo, chalking up another failure of communication.

Unaware, Hari smiled reminiscently. 'He has always been interested, since he was a child. It was the subject he studied at his English university. For a while he even threatened his father he would make it his profession.' He laughed. 'His father had not spoken to him for a year. But when he heard that, he summoned him to the Palace at once. But I'm sorry to bore you. His Excellency must have told you this already.'

The nightmare pressed closer. His Excellency, Leo was beginning to realise, had told her precisely nothing about himself.

'N-no.'

Hari thought hard thoughts about Amer. How on earth was this woman going to deal with the seething politics of Dalmun without some background? It was like sending a tourist into the desert without a compass.

He set himself to repair the omission as best he could in the remaining hours of the flight.

Which was how Leo learned that Amer was the Sheikh's only surviving son and expected to take up the reins of leadership eventually. His father was passionate and volatile, however, and Amer was no obedient cipher. So they lived in separate palaces, more often than not at odds with each other.

'His Majesty is very—traditional,' Hari said, choosing his words with care. 'He does not like things to change. The ministers know that progress cannot be halted and that His Excellency recognises this. So they consult him on policy— but informally, if you follow me. Everyone looks to Sheikh Amer to persuade his father to improve things. But, of course, in the end it is always His Majesty's decision.'

'It sounds appalling,' said Leo from the heart. 'Responsibility without power. The pits. Especially if he is fond of his father.'

Hari looked at her in quick surprise. Not many of Amer's friends had understood that. None of the girl-friends that he could remember had come anywhere near appreciating Amer's dilemma. He suddenly felt a lot more hopeful.

'You are so right,' he agreed with enthusiasm. He became less correct. And a good deal less discreet. 'It's a real tightrope. His father is unpredictable. For example, last year he confined Amer to house arrest for a while when he refused to marry again.'

Leo froze.

Hari did not notice. 'We were all afraid,' he went on. 'But then someone presented him with a wild caught saker falcon and he insisted that Amer went on a hunting trip with him to try it out. And when they came back, all their disagreements were forgotten. Amer was allowed to go to Egypt just as if they had never had a disagreement.' He shrugged helplessly.

'Was that when I met him?' Leo said hollowly. 'After he'd just come out of house arrest?'

'Yes.'

'And just because he did not want to marry again?'

Hari was rueful. 'You must understand that there is a lot of tribal unrest in Dalmun. Officially we do not admit it but in practice there are several tribes—particularly some of desert Bedouins—who are dissatisfied with the part they are allowed to play in government. Amer wants to deal with this by negotiation but his father thinks that another family alliance is all that is needed.'

'I don't understand.'

'Amer's first wife came from a powerful border family,' he explained. 'They used to make trouble regularly. But ever since the marriage they have sided with His Majesty. Even after she died—' He stopped. Leo had flinched. 'What is it?' he said in concern.

'I didn't know.' Her mouth felt stiff. The words sounded strange. 'How did she die? Was it recent?'

Hari was shocked. Damn it, what was Amer doing with this girl?

He said reassuringly, 'It was years ago. Amer was still at university.'

'What was she like?'

Hari shrugged. It was years since he had thought about the spoilt beauty that Amer had married.

'I didn't really know her. I was very young. She was very beautiful, very fashionable.'

Leo's heart sank like a stone.

'How did she die? Was she ill?'

'No, nothing like that. It was an accident. She was thrown from a horse. Somewhere in France I believe.'

'How terrible,' she whispered.

Hari was startled. Then uncomfortable. 'It was a long time ago,' he said again. 'I do not think Amer is still grieving. I've never heard him mention her.'

'But he did not marry again,' Leo said. 'If it was so long ago you would have expected him to fall in love again, wouldn't you?'

She could imagine all too vividly how the death of his young wife must have struck him to the core. She felt desolate at the thought.

Hari saw he had made a mistake and did not know how to retrieve it. He pushed a harassed hand through his hair.

'Oh, he has not been short of love,' he said unwisely. 'There was just no reason for him to marry.'

Leo gave him a stricken look. He could have kicked himself.

'Look,' he said desperately, 'don't get the wrong idea. In Dalmun marriage is a strategic thing. For everyone involved. It is all very practical. Don't start thinking of Amer as some tragic, grief-stricken hero. He isn't.'

Leo did not answer.

So why had Amer accepted her vainglorious challenge? Why had he pursued her? She had thought she had the answer. Pride! But in that case why, when he had defeated her in every way there was, why was he still insisting that they were engaged in spite of her denials?

Well, now she had the answer to that, too. He did not want to make one of those practical, strategic marriages. Probably he was still in love with his tragically dead wife. He wanted her as high-class camouflage, to keep his father at bay when he pressed him to marry again.

Leo flayed herself with the thought.

Oh, there were other elements, of course. Amer, she knew by now, wanted to win any game he played. When she slipped away from Cairo without leaving him a message she must have felt for a moment that he had lost that game. He would not have tolerated that, hence the private investigators.

And there was sex of course. Leo's experience might be limited. But she realised that the sexual current between her and Amer was powerful by any standards. He would not want to leave that unexplored. She shivered, remembering.

Hari said that Amer had not been short of love. She believed him—if love was what you called it. Those lazy, laughing kisses. The unhurried touch. Even that final glinting triumph. They all spoke of a man who knew exactly what he was doing. Skill like that, thought Leo wincing, only came with practice.

She could feel the heat in her cheeks. Oh it was effective, all right. It might not have much to do with love but a woman could forget that in the intoxication of those moments in his arms.

Her memories were too graphic. She banished them, resolutely. It was as well she did. Hari's confidences had become crucial.

'Everyone thought he would not marry again after all this time. Your news will be a great joy to everyone.'

Leo gaped. Hari smiled reassuringly and, quite unconsciously, added the final drop to her cup of despair.

'His Majesty will come round in time. You'll see.'

In London Amer was in his final and most important meeting. It was not one his father knew anything about, although both the Finance Ministry and the Department of Health had contributed to the paper under discussion. There were four men on the other side of the table.

'It is all very well,' said a dark, angry man. 'But why is it taking so long?'

'You know why, Saeed,' said one of his companions patiently. 'This time it will be different.'

'Because Sheikh Amer will pretend that these things are needed for his excavation.' The man was contemptuous. 'Why is the truth not enough? Our people have poor water and no electricity. Dalmun is not a poor country. We have oil, minerals. And His Majesty buys racehorses and bits of foreign industry! It is an outrage.'

Privately Amer agreed with him. He was too loyal to his father to say so, however.

Instead he said soothingly, 'Well, as you see from the papers in front of you, the electricity infrastructure will start to be installed next month. After that we start to implement the water conservation project.'

Saeed was not soothed. He was the only man in the room in flowing traditional dress. It kept tangling round the legs of the hotel chairs, as he kicked his feet in frustration.

He said mutinously, 'We have been waiting too long. People have stopped believing Sheikh Amer's promises.'

There was a chorus of protest from the other three. Saeed seemed to take confidence from it. He stopped wrestling with his robes.

'I warn you,' he said directly to Amer. 'There will be action.'

Amer broke into the outcry.

'What sort of action?' he said softly.

Saeed's expression became shifty. He shrugged. 'They don't tell me. I am too far away. But there will be something.'

'Another kidnapping?' Amer said lightly. 'I'm told it's starting to be offered as an exciting option for adventurous tourists.' His eyes were watchful.

'It is no joke to people who get sick from bad water,' said Saeed hotly.

'And I am not laughing at them,' Amer said at once. 'But is it sensible to deal with modern problems by thirteenth-century strategies?'

Saeed looked at him with dislike. 'Maybe we should be more *focused*,' he said mockingly.

Amer stiffened.

But Saeed's colleagues shouted him down so loudly that Amer judged it diplomatic not to pursue the subject. He did not forget it, though. As soon as he came out of his meeting he called Dalmun with an urgent message.

And then he gave instructions to the crew of the private jet which had been on stand-by all day.

A car with screened windows met Leo at the airport. Hari assured her it was to protect them from the sun but Leo was not convinced. It felt as if she were being kept out of sight. Though, when it was Amer himself who insisted on her coming to his country, she could not imagine why. She said so.

'Not at all,' said Hari.

He was sweating silently. It was not the first time he had adapted the truth to suit Amer's purposes. But, under Leo's sceptical gaze, he found it amazingly difficult to sustain. The gorgeous Julie in Cannes had been a lot easier to deal with, he thought.

As instructed, he took her to Amer's palace in the foothills.

'You will be pleased with it,' he said pleadingly. 'Amer inherited it from his grandfather and he has kept it traditional. The sunken garden and the courtyard with the fountains are exactly as they have been for centuries. For the rest—well he put in electricity and some modern plumbing, that's all.'

It was dark by the time they reached the palace. Pushing aside the curtains, Leo saw great wooden gates open silently. They were set in pale walls that must twenty feet high, she thought.

'It's a fortress,' she said, taken aback.

Just for a moment she thought she caught a glimpse of a mountain ridge against the starlit sky. But then they swept into the courtyard and there were too many people for her to concentrate on the landscape. They surrounded the car with greetings and offers of service.

In spite of the vocabulary Leo had picked up in Egypt, their Arabic was too rapid or too accented for her to follow. She turned to Hari. She had the feeling that all was not well. It made her feel helpless. She did not like it.

Hari assimilated the information fast and, although he hardly reacted at all, Leo was convinced that her suspicions were right.

'What is it?' she said in quick concern.

But he was smiling, saying it was nothing, a few administrative matters only. She would be tired after her journey. She would want to rest. A room had been prepared for her in the women's quarters. Fatima, who spoke English, would show her the way and fetch her a light supper if she required it.

Leo smiled at Fatima, who had gentle eyes and was looking excited by their arrival. But all her instincts told her that something was wrong.

She said sharply, 'Has there been a message from Amer?'

'Yes indeed,' said Hari. 'He will be here tomorrow afternoon.'

Relieved to be able to tell the truth, he beamed at Leo. She distrusted him deeply. But he was right in one thing at least. After her sleepless night, and the conflicting emotions of the last twenty-four hours, she was exhausted.

So she let Fatima conduct her to a cool, vaulted room. The leaded windows looked out onto a skyline of palm trees. Above them, the stars seemed to quiver with the intensity of their light. A new moon curved like a scimitar slash above the horizon.

She opened the window and leaned out. The scent of the night rolled in at once. The smell was of heat and herbs she did not know. Leo suddenly felt very small and alien. And alone. She shivered.

There was a touch on her arm. She looked round, startled.

Fatima was offering her a small porcelain cup of some golden liquid. It was steaming. Her eyes were kind.

'Sheikh Amer will be here tomorrow,' she said comfortingly.

For no reason that Leo could think of, she found her eyes filling with tears. She dashed them away angrily. Tiredness, she thought. That was all it was. The mere presence of Amer—or anybody else for that matter—was not enough to make her feel at home in an alien land. That took time and patience and study; and depended entirely on the effort she put into it herself. Amer was irrelevant.

But it would clearly have been a waste of time to tell this to Fatima. So she shrugged and let herself be shown the beauties of the suite which the Sheikh had ordered to be prepared for her. Apart from the bedroom, there was a bathroom that could rival any she had seen in the most luxurious hotels in the world, a sitting room furnished with exquisitely carved furniture and strewn with jewel-coloured cushions, and a small roof terrace. The terrace was triangular and at its apex there was a statue of a falcon with its beak open.

'When the wind blows, the falcon breathes,' Fatima explained poetically. 'There is a legend...'

But Leo's eyelids were drooping. Fatima was sympathetic. She made sure that Leo had everything she needed and left.

Leo wanted to think but she could not. She fell into a bed. And a sleep too deep for dreams.

In the morning, of course, it was different. She awoke with a start, her heart pounding. At first she did not know where she was and the leaded lights in the window looked like prison bars. But then she saw the doors open to the terrace, with full daylight streaming in, and she remembered. She sank back among the pillows with a gasp of relief.

It was quickly succeeded by all the doubts that had beset her yesterday. Where was she? With the curtains closed she had not really been able to detect much of the route they had taken from the palace. Hari had taken charge of everything, including her passport. The prison analogy did not seem so far-fetched after all.

She pulled on yesterday's clothes and went to look for

someone, anyone. She needed to assert that it was she—not Amer and certainly not Hari—who was in charge of her life.

She found them easily enough. Asserting herself was more difficult. For one thing, everyone denied knowledge of Hari's current whereabouts.

'Perhaps he has gone to the airport to meet the Sheikh,' Fatima suggested helpfully.

She was delighted to bring Leo food. She attended assiduously to her comfort. She showed her round the palace and its shaded gardens. And when Leo grew restive, she introduced her to a quiet scholarly man who laid out books and maps and the Sheikh's archaeological finds for her admiration until Leo thought she would scream.

'Look,' she said dangerously, 'I'm not interested in His Excellency's leisure activities.'

'I hope you don't mean that,' said a voice from the doorway. An amused voice. One, she now realised, that had whispered through her dreamless sleep.

She swung round and yelled at him, 'Don't you laugh at me. Don't you *dare* laugh at me.'

Her quiet companion folded maps and retreated rapidly.

'You've embarrassed Hussein,' said Amer reproachfully.

Leo was shaking. With fury she told herself.

'Never mind Hussein. Where is Hari? And what has he done with my passport?' she burst out.

Amer blinked.

'And welcome home to you, too,' he said drily. 'Yes thank you, the flight was quite pleasant.'

'I don't care what sort of flight you had,' shouted Leo, thoroughly upset. 'I want to get out of here.'

Amer sat down on the other side of ancient map table and folded his hands together into a pyramid. He regarded her thoughtfully. 'Why?'

'*Why?*' Leo glared. 'Isn't it obvious? Nobody likes being held a prisoner.'

Amer remained calm.

'And what has convinced you that you're a prisoner?'

She made a despairing gesture. 'I don't know where I am. Nobody will tell me anything. They just say to wait for you. And they took my passport away.' To her dismay, her voice choked on this last statement. She looked away.

'I see.' He sounded unforgivably calm. 'Do you want to run away so soon?'

Leo rummaged in her trouser pocket for a handkerchief and failed to find one. She sniffed as unobtrusively as she could.

'I want to be in control of my own affairs,' she said when she thought she had mastered her voice again.

There was a pause which she could not interpret.

'A modern woman,' he teased. 'My father will be shocked.'

Leo raised her head, arrested. 'Your father?'

'We are having dinner with him,' Amer told her gravely.

Leo's heart fluttered in her breast. 'A-are we?' she said, uncertain all of a sudden.

He gave her that terrible, tender, deceiving smile. 'Unless you'd rather take your passport and go, of course.'

Leo wanted to demand her passport and sweep out of the room immediately. At the same time, she wanted him to take her in his arms and tell her that he loved her—and that he wanted her never to leave his side. It was not *fair*.

Amer sensed her dilemma, it seemed. He stood up and strolled over to an intricately carved cabinet. He opened a small drawer and extracted a little booklet. It was, Leo saw with indignation, not even locked. Amer tossed the passport across to her.

'There you are, my darling. Your freedom, if you want it,' he said with irony.

Leo caught it out of the air, like a starving monkey fielding falling fruit. She clutched it to her breast protectively. Amer's irony deepened.

'So am I to order the car to take you to the airport?'

To her own complete astonishment Leo heard herself say, 'No.'

His eyes lifted; lit with a wicked light.

'Ah.'

'If your father is kind enough to ask me to dinner, it is only polite to go,' she said with dignity.

'Oh, absolutely,' he said, smooth as silk.

She was sure her colour rose. To disguise it, she looked at her watch in her most efficient manner. 'Of course, I shall need time to get ready. I'm not sure whether I've brought anything suitable to wear. I wasn't expecting to come to Dalmun when I packed.'

He smiled. 'I can advise you.'

Leo had a sudden vivid picture of him, inspecting the clothes that Fatima had unpacked for her this morning. Padding around in her bedroom, no doubt as if he owned it. Which of course he did. Her breathing quickened.

'I think I can manage to sort something out on my own, thanks.'

Amer's eyes danced. 'But you will need advice on local conventions of dress.'

'I'll ask Fatima,' Leo said firmly. She was sure her colour was hectic.

He laughed and flung up his hands in a gesture of surrender.

'I will tell her that you are to borrow anything you require.'

Leo recoiled. 'Borrow! From whom?'

Was he suggesting she wear his wife's clothes? Was this where he told her about his wife at last? Suddenly she did not want to hear about his love for another woman.

He eyed her speculatively. 'I have guests from time to time. We are out of town here. It is not always possible for them to buy what they need at a moment's notice. So we keep a few spare clothes for visitors to borrow if necessary.' He read her mind again. 'Men as well as women,' he added kindly.

This time there was no doubt. Leo flushed scarlet. She could feel it.

He laughed again, quite differently.

'You look agitated. You should rest.'

'On the contrary,' she said with as much dignity as she could muster. 'I slept too long.'

'Then you have not recovered from the journey yet,' he said imperturbably. 'As I have not myself. Let us rest together.'

There was a shattering silence, broken only by the thump of her heart. Leo thought: He didn't say that. He *can't* have said that. He can't think I'm here to fall into bed with him when he snaps his fingers.

But Hari had said, 'He wasn't short of love.' And she had already fallen into bed with him, hadn't she? It was no thanks to her that they were not already lovers in all the ways there were.

Amer held out his hand.

She said harshly, 'You can't be serious. That is such a cliché.'

He was not put out. 'I merely suggest what we both want. Where is the cliché in that?' The grey eyes were warm.

Leo closed her eyes against the allure. If she did not look at him, she would be able to stick to her resolve.

'It's feudal.'

'And are you so modern?'

His voice was a caress. It set little shivers of desire rippling through every nerve ending. Oh, she could close her eyes and maybe her ears but he was in her bloodstream now and her whole body ached to turn to him. It wasn't *fair*.

She said, 'I don't believe in casual sex.'

He said nothing. Cautiously Leo opened her eyes.

Amer had folded his arms and propped himself up negligently against the corner of the table. He did not try to touch her. But he looked as if he was happy to stay there and debate with her forever. Or until she gave in.

'What sort of sex do you believe in?' he said in an interested voice.

Leo was thrown off balance. As, no doubt, he had intended, though she did not realise that until too late. Mistakenly she tried to answer him.

'Oh, when two people know each other. When they—'

'We know each other,' he murmured.

She glared. 'When they have spent time together and know each other's faults and reached a rational decision—'

He was disbelieving. 'Rational?'

'Of course.'

He shook his head. 'You are even weirder than I thought. What has reason to do with love?'

'Love,' said Leo contemptuously.

'Oh don't modern women believe in love, either?'

'We'll leave my beliefs out of it.'

'Running away again,' he said softly.

Leo's temper surged. 'Are you trying to tell me that you brought me here because you *love* me?' she flashed.

Amer stretched lazily. But his eyes were watchful.

'Is it so impossible?'

'You made me a *prisoner*,' Leo pointed out. 'Not very loving, that.'

'But we are all prisoners when we love,' Amer said soulfully.

Leo sent him a look of acute dislike.

'Don't keep talking about love. It makes me sick. You brought me here because you can't bear to lose a game,' she flung at him. 'Any game, however trivial. And I was winning, wasn't I? Until I got emotional and handed it to you on a plate.'

For a moment he did not answer. Then he said slowly, 'You are a very untrusting woman.'

'I'm a realistic woman. What grounds have I got for trusting you?'

Amer was rather pale. He unfolded his length from the carved table and came towards her.

He said, not laughing at all, 'But I told you I would marry you.'

'And you did not tell me that you had been married before,' Leo flung back at him.

He stopped dead.

'Is it true?'

All of a sudden, his eyes were quite opaque.

'Yes.'

She shrugged, though her heart was screaming with pain.
'My case proved, don't you think?'

She walked out of the room. He did not try to stop her.

CHAPTER NINE

THE cupboards in the guest quarters yielded up an infinite range of clothes for Leo to choose from: long dark robes that would cover her from head to toe, brilliant silks that would cover as much or as little as she wished, cotton, linen, lawn, even gold-encrusted brocade.

'Minister of Culture strikes again, I take it,' Leo muttered.

She selected a simple robe with a long overjacket in pea-cock silk. Fatima nodded approval and fetched her a heavy gold collar, like elegant chain-mail, and several intricate bangles to go with it.

'No,' said Leo, revolted.

She was not wearing Amer's wife's jewellery for anything.

Fatima was agitated. She did not have enough English to make Leo understand and ran out of the room. Leo felt slightly ashamed but she could not bear the idea of putting the heavy thing against her skin.

The heavy doors to her room banged back. Amer strode in, looking irritated.

'*Now* what are you making a fuss about?' he said in tones of barely controlled exasperation.

'I may have to borrow clothes but I'm not wearing some-one else's jewels.'

Amer flicked a bored glance over the gold collar.

'They're yours,' he said curtly.

'No they're not.' Leo was nearly dancing with rage.

'Of course they are.' He flicked back the lid of the jew-ellery box for her to see the name of the Paris jeweller. 'A gift for my future wife. Flown in today.'

Leo was utterly taken aback.

'You bought me a *necklace?*'

149

'Of course.' He shrugged, bored. 'It's a trifle. We will, of course, choose your betrothal gift together.'

Leo sat down rather suddenly.

'But—I can't accept—'

Even to her own ears, she sounded like a confused child.

'I advise you to swallow your pride.' He sounded irritated. 'My father is asking other women to dinner tonight, as a courtesy to you. You will find them heavily jewelled. You will feel very odd if you aren't.'

He did not sound, though, as if he cared very much. And he did not give her a kiss or a kind look to go with the ornaments. Leo felt chilled and angry and would have said so forcefully but Fatima came back.

Amer smiled at her gently. *He did not smile at me,* thought Leo desolate.

He said something to her which made Fatima bow her head and give a small well-behaved giggle. And then he strode out. He said not one word more to Leo.

Leo was tempted to scream, but she gave up the idea when she saw how relieved Fatima was that she had given in over the gold necklace. Fatima was, Leo realised, quite seriously flustered by the fact that Amer was taking Leo to dine with his father. She did not have enough English to explain why. Leo could think of plenty of reasons.

She flung them at Amer when they got into the long dark car without number plates.

'Tell me,' she said chattily, 'does your father usually meet your playmates?'

'Do not speak of yourself like that.'

It was a command. Leo glared. But she did not quite dare to challenge him.

Amer was looking more of a stranger than ever tonight. He wore a loose jacket, heavily embroidered in crimson and turquoise, over his white robe. And there was a wicked looking dagger, the size of a small sword, in his belt. But it was not just his clothes. His mouth was set in forbidding lines and his eyes were strained. He looked like a diplomat going to a negotiation that could end in war.

Was meeting his father always so fraught? Leo thought. Or was it her presence that gave him that wary look?

'Will your father put me under house arrest for daring to lay hands on his son and heir?' she said provocatively.

Amer sent her an unsmiling look. 'I see Hari has been talking.'

'Unlike you.'

His jaw tightened. 'Don't try to make me angry, Leonora. We will talk, I promise. But now is not the time.'

'Great,' she muttered.

But they were at tall iron gates which swung wide as soon as the car nosed onto the approach road. Beside her, she could feel Amer straighten as if he was bracing himself.

Leo felt a brief remorse. It was soon dispelled.

'My father will ask you about our relationship,' he said rapidly. 'I advise you to tell him nothing.'

'Would he punish you for kidnapping me?'

A muscle worked in his cheek. 'I did not,' he said evenly, 'kidnap you.'

'Will your father believe that?'

He swung round on her, his eyes cool. 'Tell him and see,' he invited.

Leo's eyes narrowed. 'Why?'

He gave a crack of unamused laughter. 'He won't blame me. He is more likely to put you under house arrest until you marry me.'

It was like being doused in cold water. Leo sank back, silenced.

His father was not as tall as Amer but the gold on his robes made him seem somehow bigger. He had a grizzled beard and fierce, suspicious eyes. He spoke to Leo in rusty French which was courteous rather than welcoming.

They ate out of doors in a cool courtyard. A heavy oaken table, set with gleaming glass and china, was placed under a curved canopy. Behind them, the walls of the palace were white stone, warm to the touch. In front of them, date palms rustled in the evening breeze. Their leaves made a sound like rain, vying with the delicate tinkling of fountains.

'An informal supper,' said Amer. 'My father thought you would find that easier.'

'Informal?'

The King sat in a heavy oak chair with carved arms and a high back. It was as near to a throne as damn it, thought Leo. And there were at least twenty other people at the table.

Amer gave a taut smile. 'Just close family.'

Even so, everyone she met seemed to be a Minister or a Minister's wife.

Leo found that she was swept off to the end of the table to eat with the women. One or two wore what were clearly Paris designs but most, like herself, wore long robes. And Amer was right. To a woman, traditionally dressed or not, they all wore magnificent jewellery. But they were friendly and surprisingly sympathetic.

'Amer is a law unto himself,' said a pretty cousin.

'Always was,' said an aunt by marriage. She was wearing a stunningly simple black cocktail dress and sapphires.

'And so impetuous,' sighed a middle-aged woman with laughing eyes. She wore a gold encrusted smoking jacket and earrings like Baccarat chandeliers.

'Are you related to the Minister of Culture by any chance?' murmured Leo, eyeing the gold lapels with fascination.

'My brother.'

'Ah.'

'*He* says that Amer is the only one who is holding Dalmun together,' confided the Minister's wife. 'His Majesty is so very traditional. It is a heavy burden for Amer, especially as he has been alone for so long.'

Leo was not deceived by the airy tone. She winced.

'He told you,' she said, resigned.

'Told? In Dalmun? You're joking. Just rumours that you are, er, close. And—' She broke off.

'And?'

The Minister's wife leaned forward confidentially. 'And Amer not being able to keep his eyes off you.'

Leo looked down the table. Amer was sitting on his father's right, immersed in conversation. He was frowning slightly, tearing at the flat bread with preoccupied fingers, not eating any of it. As if he felt her eyes on him, he looked up suddenly.

Leo caught her breath. For a moment it was as if there was just the two of them. The cheerful conversation faded into nothing. She just stared and stared.

Take me away. Come down the table and take me home and make love to me.

It was so strong a wish that she almost felt as if she had said it aloud. She saw his eyes grow intent. His hands cast the maltreated bread away impatiently. But then his father said something, put a hand on his arm, and the moment was broken.

Leo sank back in her chair with a little gasp. Her pulse was racing. And deep, deep inside she felt a hollow need stir.

Afterwards, when he helped her into the car, she could feel the heat of his hands. Sitting close together in the back of the car was a torment. She was conscious of him, taut muscles hot and hard, and knew that the chauffeur and Amer's public image made him as out of reach as the moon.

When they arrived Amer waved the car away. In the sudden silence of the well-lit entrance, he stood in front of her for a moment, as if undecided.

Leo thought, *he's going to kiss me.* But he did not. Instead he leaned forward until his cheek just touched her hair.

'I will come to you later.' His voice was a rough whisper. 'May I?'

'Yes,' breathed Leo.

But he did not. She waited for hours in the strange room, moving restlessly from table to balcony and back. The night wind was cold. But not as cold as the lonely bed.

He did not come and he sent no message.

* * *

'I don't believe this,' said Amer.

'Your father wants you back at the palace,' Hari repeated. 'A report has just come in. Brigands on the northern border.'

'Brigands!' Amer was scornful. 'More likely tribesmen who want decent water and a telephone line for their village.'

'Your father wants to send in the Army…'

Amer swore.

'All right,' he said at last. 'I'll go. But if I'm not back in an hour—' He broke off.

'Yes?'

'*Hell,*' said Amer.

In the end the apricot light of early dawn slid along the balustrade of the balcony before Leo huddled down on the sofa and did what she could to sleep. That was where Fatima found her. She had not even taken off last night's finery. The chain-mail necklace had marked her skin.

'Typical,' said Leo, refusing to cry.

Fatima was concerned. Particularly when Leo took off Sheikh Amer's gift and threw it so hard across the room that a link broke. Even more so when Leo refused to wear any more of the borrowed clothes.

'I shall buy something myself. The car can take me to the market, can't it?'

Fatima was uneasy. She began to mutter, losing her command of English.

'Or am I a prisoner here after all?' demanded Leo, savagely triumphant.

Fatima bit her lip and consulted Hari. They both strove strenuously to dissuade her.

'Sheikh Amer said you were to have whatever you ask for,' Hari told Leo at last. It clearly troubled him. 'It would be wiser not to go to the market today, though.'

'So I *am* a prisoner.'

He gave in, stipulating only that she took an escort. Leo set off in triumph accompanied by the scholarly map reader.

He looked rather alarmed. Leo interpreted it as a sign that he did not know much about women's clothes.

'It's all right,' she told him. 'We'll be back before sundown.'

'You'll be back in two hours,' said Hari firmly.

Leo went very still. 'Is that how long you've got before Amer wakes up and finds out you've let me go?'

Exasperated, Hari said, 'Be careful. Dalmun is not Knightsbridge.'

But Leo waved a careless hand and he stepped back. The electric gates opened silently and the limousine swept through.

'I hope I've done the right thing,' said Hari aloud.

Three hours later, his heart in his mouth, he was knocking on the door to Amer's suite.

'Come in.'

Amer was at his desk. It was clear from the table strewn with paper behind him that he had been working, not resting. He looked up.

'Have you been to bed at all?' said Hari, shocked by his look of exhaustion.

Amer shook his head. 'What time is it?'

Hari told him. He was startled.

'So late? Then I must see—' He broke off.

But Hari was beyond pretending to be discreet.

'She's gone,' he said brutally.

Amer stared at him. His face was masklike. Hari could not bear it.

'Not of her own accord. Hussein came back with a message. Oh, I knew I should never have let her go.'

Amer went very still.

'Go? Where?'

'She insisted on going out,' said poor Hari. 'I tried to persuade her— But you told her she was free to do whatever she wanted. And this morning she was like a caged animal.'

Amer flinched. Hari did not notice.

'I insisted that Hussein went along to interpret. But he is not a man of action. Saeed's people have taken her. They sent Hussein back. They want your father to sign the order for the new electricity system at the Council Meeting tomorrow.'

Amer looked at him for a burning moment.

'They'll keep her until he does,' Hari finished miserably. 'I'm sorry, Amer. I know you warned us. But it never occurred to me they would really do it. They've only ever taken an ordinary tourist before.'

Amer said. 'Get my father on the telephone.'

Hari blanched. 'What are you going to do?'

'Tell him the truth,' said Amer harshly. 'I have protected him from it for too long. Let him know that some of his subjects will turn against him unless he gives them a reasonable standard of living.'

'Very well.' Hari did not relish the task but he was a brave man. 'Do you want me to call your uncle and summon the Council?'

'That is for my father to decide,' said Amer. 'It's his Council.'

'But—'

'They will have taken her into the desert. I'm going after her. Get the land cruiser ready.'

Hari was startled into an undiplomatic truth. 'But you have to go to the Council. They will never be able to persuade His Majesty without you. They need you.'

'Leonora needs me.'

Amer was already opening cupboards, his mind on his expedition.

Hari was exasperated. 'But you've said it yourself often enough—these guys are harmless. She's in no danger. They'll probably give her the time of her life.'

Amer said, 'Does Leonora know that?'

'Well maybe not to begin with,' he admitted. 'But she'll find out…'

'Or she might not. Saeed is different from the other desert Sheikhs. More ambitious. Definitely more unpredictable.'

'He would not hurt her,' said Hari positively. 'It would be stupid.'

Amer turned. He looked strained.

'My head agrees with you. My heart can't take the chance.'

His heart? *Amer's* heart? Hari stared in disbelief.

'But why?' he said incautiously.

The smile became savage.

'Because she's *mine*.'

Leo was afraid. She told herself that Amer would find her. She told herself to believe her captors when they assured her that she was their honoured guest. But it was difficult when they sounded so terrifyingly efficient.

As they got farther and farther from the capital and left the metalled road for a dust track, her heart sank. Even with the windows closed, the dust seemed to whirl chokingly round the interior of the cabin.

The tropic dark fell like a blanket. The pick-up stopped. The driver got out. After a few minutes he came back and gestured Leo to get out of the vehicle.

All her banked-down panic surged up into her throat. She could taste it. Were they going to abandon her here, in the middle of nowhere? Amer would never find her, then.

She controlled herself. Amer did what he set himself to do. Besides this was his country. And anyway, she just knew that he would find her. Of course he would find her.

Leo hugged that thought to her. It got her through the next few hours. And she really needed something to hold on to because her captors seemed as if they did not know what to do with her. She was transferred from vehicle to vehicle no fewer than four times and, judging from the limited Arabic she had picked up in Cairo, none of the men taking charge of her was glad of the responsibility. Leo began to feel like a potato that had just been pulled out of the fire: too hot to handle. And the later it got, the jumpier each successive group of men sounded.

Eventually the last truck pulled up at a group of tents. They were hunched shadows under the brilliant sky. Leo stumbled out. She was swaying with tiredness as much as emotion.

They took her into an enormous tent with all ceremony, fed her coffee and speeches which she could not understand, then took her to a smaller tent where she tried to sleep.

She dreamed that Amer's arms were round her. And woke up with tears on her cheeks.

All through the morning Leo heard comings and goings in the main tent. She tried to stay calm but it was not easy. She drank a little water but refused all food. Eventually an impatient man arrived bearing a circular dish of bread and fruit. Leo shook her head but he took no notice, pressing bread against her lips. Leo shut her eyes so she should not see his expression. It was menacing.

Oh, Amer, get me out of this, she called silently.

There was a commotion outside. The man flung the tray away and stamped out.

Leo sipped some water, shakily. He had gripped her arm in his attempt to make her eat and the place throbbed. There would be a bruise there, she thought.

Soon enough he was back and abandoning other attempts at communication, hauling her into the main tent. Leo fought down another sick surge of panic. She had to keep her head, she knew.

The main tent was full of men. They all had their backs to her, looking at an imposing figure in the entrance to the tent.

For all her determined courage, Leo's heart contracted. Was this a gathering of rebel clans?

The man in the bright mouth of the tent seemed very tall. He wore a flowing black robe and turban. It made him look like the angel of death. His face was in complete shadow but Leo could see the arrogance in the way he held himself.

Was he cruel, too? The others were clearly in awe of him.

No, thought Leo watching the way they bowed to him, not in awe. Make that terrified. She felt her mouth dry with a reflection of their terror.

He was unaware of her. He said something to the bowing reception committee. His voice was harsh. He took a step forward and the robe proved to be a loose coat, the open front heavy with gold embroidery. It flashed in the sun. Under it he wore some dark shirt with a huge plaited leather belt worked in gold stretching from waist to slim hips. And he had a huge dagger, its blade a wicked upcurve. The sheath looked like pure gold and its haft was set with jewels. It was magnificent and utterly barbarian.

Even though she could not see his face, Leo saw that this was a leader. She felt a flash of terror, pure and primitive. She must have made some sound. The man turned his fierce attention to the far side of the tent where she was standing.

He strode forward. She caught a glimpse of high boots. And the gold flashed dazzlingly. She was terrified. She shut her eyes.

The man took hold of her chin. 'Are you all right?' he said in clipped, furious English.

Disbelieving, Leo looked up. It was Amer. But not Amer as she had ever seen him before. There was no laughter in the grey eyes that swept over her and barely any recognition. Amer was a brisk stranger on important business. His whole manner said that she was a major nuisance.

Inwardly she cringed. Aloud she said sharply, 'I'm fine. No thanks to—'

'Stop right there,' he said softly. He sounded so angry he could barely speak. 'I'll handle this. Keep your mouth *shut.*'

Leo fumed. But all her survival instincts told her to comply. So she folded her lips together and glared.

Amer turned back to their hosts.

'I am grateful to you for finding her,' he said formally. She could understand his Arabic more easily. 'The lady is a treasured guest and new to our country.'

He was not just formal, Leo thought. He was glacial. The

other men shuffled uncomfortably. It was clear, even to Leo, that for the time being Sheikh Amer was willing to pretend that the girl had just stumbled into their camp. But if they did not hand her over he was quite prepared to take her by whatever means were necessary. The unspoken threat of force hung heavy in the air.

Leo was not proud of herself for the feeling. But she was glad of the strong body between her and the rest of the tent's occupants.

'One wonders how such an honoured guest managed to get lost in the desert,' said one of the younger men defiantly.

He attracted fulminating looks from his companions. Amer contented himself with inspecting the man in nerve-racking silence for a full minute.

'One does indeed,' he said softly.

His tone made even Leo's blood run cold.

There was a general hubbub of disclaimers. The man looked mutinous but others, older and more cautious, were delivering a confused and contradictory account of how she arrived at the camp. It was not clear whether they expected to be believed. Amer made little pretence at believing them, in any event.

Above the hum his voice could be heard announcing, 'As my future wife she is doubly precious.'

It sounded, thought Leo writhing, more like a declaration of war than love. Of course, he did not realise that she could understand him. She folded her lips together and promised herself that he would never know. Once they were out of this she would never refer to it again. Never.

But it had its desired effect. They did not exactly congratulate him. But they surrendered her into his custody with every evidence of relief. After more ceremonial coffee drinking and expressions of eternal fidelity on both sides, they were escorted to a massive four-wheel drive vehicle.

'Not a camel?' said Leo mockingly. 'It would go better with the outfit.'

It was the first time she had spoken. Amer turned a look

on her which, if they had detected it, would have caused their hosts to doubt that she was so precious in their Sheikh's eyes. A muscle worked at his jaw. He looked as if he could cheerfully have murdered her.

'Not a word,' he said between his teeth. 'Not one more word. Or you'll wish you had never been born.'

'What makes you think I don't already?' muttered Leo.

But he had turned away and was making their farewells.

He drove off, his face set. He handled the big land cruiser with an easy mastery which Leo somehow would not have expected. For so much of their acquaintance they had been driven by chauffeurs, she thought. This coolly competent driving in difficult terrain reminded her—if she needed to be reminded—how little she really knew Amer.

She said in a small voice, 'Where are we going?'

'My camp,' he said briefly.

He looked at a dial mounted in the dash. With a slight shock, Leo realised it was a compass, not a decorative addition to an expensive car but a real float mounted compass. She swallowed.

'Is the desert very dangerous?'

'If you don't know it. Or if you are careless.' He sent her an ironic look. 'Why? Were you thinking of setting out across the desert in your high heels if I didn't come to rescue you?'

Leo thought: I am going to cry. All that time in captivity and I didn't shed a tear and now, when I'm safe, I could bawl like a baby. It was because he was so angry with her, of course. And because, in part, he had cause.

And because he would not be that angry if he loved her.

She swallowed something jagged in her throat and said, 'I never thought you would come to rescue me.'

'Oh? You thought I would leave you to Saeed's mercy?' He sounded furious.

This was horrible. Floundering Leo said, 'I mean I never thought you would come yourself. I knew you would not just abandon me, of course. But...'

'You thought I would send someone else to do my dirty work,' he interpreted.

Not just furious. Savage.

Leo said nastily, so that she would not cry, 'Well you set detectives after me.'

He slammed on the brakes so hard that the big vehicle skidded. Leo cried out as she was flung violently against him. Amer turned and dragged her across the control dock into his arms.

The kiss was savage.

This was not the laughing stranger who had wooed her under the Nile stars. Nor the sophisticate who had driven her to such unexpected passion in London. No unhurried love-making now. No drifting of teasing hands. This was a man way past laughter or sophistication. A man driven to the very limit of his endurance.

Leo thought: He'll never forgive me.

And then she stopped thinking altogether as desire engulfed her.

Amer twisted, slamming her body into the upholstery. Leo arched to meet him, her mouth hungry. Her jaw ached with the force of his kiss. She did to care. She heard cloth rip and did not know if it was his clothing or hers. She did not care about that, either. His fingers found her breast and she cried out in a sort of agony.

Amer gave a groan. She felt his breath in her ravaged mouth. He was too frenzied to be gentle. So was Leo. As fierce as he, she writhed against him. She needed to be closer, closer…

And he drew away. Unbelievably he drew away. Leo moaned in protest.

'No,' he bit out.

Her hands scrabbled for him. He caught them and held them strongly, holding her away from him.

'No,' he said again.

Leo was panting. She breathed in the smell of him, as familiar to her now as her own.

'You can't stop now,' she said in a ragged whisper. 'Please.'

He looked at her as if he loathed her.

'I can.' It sounded like a curse. 'I will.'

His ribs rose and fell hugely, like a ship's pump. He held himself utterly still. But Leo could see the fine tremor in his hands and knew Amer was a lot closer to losing control than he wanted to be.

She thought: *I want him to lose control.* It shocked her into immobility.

She felt dazed. It was as if she had fallen into a volcano. All right, she was out now. But she did not quite know how. Or what had been changed in the fire. Just now, it felt like everything.

Shaken, she started to wrestle with the tangle he had made of her clothes.

Staring straight ahead at the desert beyond the windscreen, Amer said, 'I'm not going to apologise.' His lips barely moved.

Leo did not answer. A button was missing from her trousers and her bra was beyond repair. Leo pulled it off and stuffed the rags into her pocket.

Amer shifted.

'That has been building up for a long time.'

Leo still said nothing. But she felt the quick look he sent her like a brand on her skin.

'For you as well as me.'

Leo flinched. He swung round on her.

'All right. I wish it hadn't happened like that,' he said in a goaded voice. 'But it was only a kiss after all. We could have—'

Then he saw her face. He drew a sharp breath. Halted.

'Damn,' he said with concentrated fury.

It was like a physical blow. Leo was remotely surprised that it was possible to feel so much pain and go on breathing.

He must not see the pain, she thought. He *must* not.

'I won't tell if you won't,' she said, quite as if she didn't care.

Evidently Amer was not taken in by her cynical tone. He sighed.

'You will see things more clearly in time.'

As if, thought Leo furiously, she was a child and he was a sage who was never, ever, wrong.

'No doubt I will. When I'm back home in London,' she retorted. And added challengingly, 'Once I've had time to put all this behind me.'

His mouth tightened. But he did not answer her. Instead he put on his sunglasses, switched on the engine and put the land cruiser in gear. As if he could not be bothered to waste time arguing with her, Leo thought. She could have screamed with frustration.

All right, she thought. If he would not speak, she would not, either. She folded her arms across her chest and stared out of her window, pointedly ignoring him.

Amer took no notice. His attention was divided between the compass and the track which unwound before them. It appeared and disappeared under drifts of dust. To their right pale dunes undulated across the horizon like lazy animals on the point of lying down to snooze. To their left, the plain of stony sand stretched away until it fell off the edge of the world in a golden dust cloud. In spite of the air-conditioning in the vehicle, Leo could almost taste the heat outside.

The road, such as it was, petered out. Amer coasted gently to a stop.

'I'll need to let some air out of the tyres.'

He swung out of the vehicle. The desert air blasted in as if he had opened the door to a furnace. Leo gasped under the impact.

Amer looked back.

'There's a bottle of water in the dash,' he said, remote but kind. 'Drink. It will take some time to get to my camp.'

It did. It was not a great journey. In spite of the land cruiser's mighty springs, Leo thought she would be sick with the uneven motion. And, although the air conditioning worked well, the hazy glare beyond the windscreen made Leo feel as if she were being grilled by aliens.

Amer was unmoved. He drove with easy competence, his body rolling with the vehicle while Leo bumped miserably from side to side.

Leo forgot that she was not speaking to him. The vastness of the desert was intimidating. It made her feel like an ant on some giant's beach.

'It's so huge,' she whispered. 'And all the same. Without that compass we could be going round in circles, wouldn't we?'

Amer smiled. 'No. This is my desert. Compass or no compass, I could get you out if I had to.'

Leo shivered. But, oddly, she found she believed him. I would trust him with my life, she thought. It was a revelation.

I am in love.

It was not a welcome revelation. She stared blankly out the window, trying to think. How long had she been in love with him? Since the evening at his London home? Before that?

And, oh horrors, did Amer know? All right, she had only just realised it. But he was so sophisticated, so infinitely more experienced than she was. Maybe he had picked it up from the first.

Leo felt sick again. And this time it was nothing to do with the motion of the vehicle. She pressed a hand to her mouth to force back a groan.

Amer looked sideways at her. 'Are you all right?'

She sought desperately for an alibi.

'Reaction setting in, I expect.' How could she sound so normal? She impressed herself. And added truthfully, 'I wasn't admitting it but I was really scared back there.'

'You did very well. Many women on their own would have lost their head.'

He sounded like a schoolmaster giving her marks in class,

she thought, irritated. It made no difference. She was still in love with him.

'Thank you,' she said drily.

'I mean it,' he said. 'I fully expected to arrive to find you screaming the place down.'

She shrugged. 'What would have been the point? It would just have annoyed them and made things ten times worse.'

He made a small, exasperated noise. 'Are you always that cool in the face of danger?'

I wasn't cool in your arms. Leo shivered inwardly at the thought. That had been danger all right. Alone in the desert with him, she realised the truth at last: She had lost her dignity, her common sense and her heart all in one massive attack. She had not seen it coming. But it had happened. Even though she had not realised it until now.

'Depends on the danger,' she said with bitter self-mockery.

Amer, she thought, was a greater risk to her peace of mind than anything her embarrassed captors had done. The only thing she could do now was keep quiet and hope that he did not find out. It would be the final humiliation if he discovered how she felt.

So she did not speak again until they got to the camp.

The first thing she saw was a black shadow. It turned out to be an enormous tent. As they got closer she made out other tents and several vehicles. They all cast shadows so deep that it looked as if a cellar had been dug in the sand beside them. Only a thin, windblown tree was not supported by a black reflection on the sand.

There was nobody in sight. It looked desolate. Leo shivered.

'Is this an oasis?'

Amer drove round the tent and parked in its sheltering shadow.

'No. It is the site of one of my excavations. We camped here because it is central to the area where we were looking for you.'

Leo looked at the shimmering dust. It was better than look-

ing at Amer. In the course of the drive, his black robe had
fallen back. She could see the smooth golden chest where
she had ripped his shirt away.

She swallowed hard and spoke entirely at random. 'Excavation? *Here?* What did you do? Shift sand from one place
to another?'

Amer laughed. 'You cannot see it because your eyes have
not accustomed themselves to the subtlety of the desert yet.
But over there are the walls of mud brick houses. In all prob-
ability they date back to the iron age.'

Leo peered at the rise of sand. It was as smooth as an egg.

'I don't see any walls.'

'The sand drifts back so quickly,' said Amer. 'I assure you
they are there. I will show you later.'

He got out of the land cruiser and came round to help her
down. The moment Leo put her hand in his, she felt that
incredible tingle, as if his very touch woke the sleeping tiger
at her body's core.

She snatched her hand away.

'I can manage, thank you.'

His mouth tightened.

'As you wish.'

The heavy gold ornamentation on the front of his robe
glinted so blindingly you could almost overlook the fact that
it gaped at the shoulder where a seam had parted in their
frenzy. The naked chest was golden as the sun and so close,
so close.

Leo's unbidden thoughts made her head swim. Hurriedly
she looked round at the other vehicles. It was only then that
she took in the size of the encampment.

'Where is everyone else?'

'Inside in the cool.'

She said curiously, 'Do you always bring such a retinue
when you come into the desert?'

She had not meant it to but it sounded faintly scornful.
Amer raised his eyebrows.

'You think I should have set out after you alone? Would that have made me more heroic in your eyes?'

Leo flinched from his sarcasm.

'Don't be ridiculous,' she said brusquely. 'I was just wondering if royalty is required to travel in convoy. To make sure everyone knows how important you are.'

He turned his head and looked at her for a long silent moment. The sun glinted off his sunglasses, masking his expression. For some reason, Leo found her chin coming up in defiance of that silent inspection, though.

'It is not wise to go alone,' Amer said at last levelly. 'It is nothing to do with being royal. We carry short wave radio and extra fuel and water. And we look out for each other.' He paused. 'Not something you high-powered business executives know much about, I think.'

It stung. As it was meant to.

Leo turned away. The heat lay on her skin like a blanket. She made for the cool of the tent without another word.

'Leonora—'

But she pretended not to hear. She did not think she could take much more without flinging herself into his arms and begging him to love her. She shuddered at the thought and kept on walking.

He caught up with her. 'I think you may prefer to go to the tent that has been prepared for you.'

She whirled, glaring. 'Is a woman not allowed to sit with the men, then?'

For a moment he looked utterly taken aback. Then he started to laugh.

'Not at all. You would be very welcome, of course. But I thought you might prefer...'

He made a graceful gesture. Leo looked down at herself. She had forgotten that her garments had suffered, too, in their mutual frenzy. Now she saw her naked breasts gleaming palely under a shirt that seemed to have lost all its buttons. She gasped and clutched the edges of material across herself.

'Come along,' he said, odiously sympathetic. 'Fatima will find you something less air cooled to wear.'

Leo took hold of the ends of her torn shirt and knotted them savagely over her midriff. Then, head high, she followed him.

CHAPTER TEN

AMER almost flung Leo into the arms of Fatima. Their approach had brought her to the entrance flap of one of the smaller tents. Her eyes widened as she took in the full enormity of Leo's ragged state.

'Deal with it.' Amer said harshly in his own language.

Leo was stricken. She turned her face away so that he should not see and swept past him without a word.

Fatima sent him an alarmed look and whisked Leo inside with little coos of concern.

'Those villains. What have they done to you?'

Leo was confused. 'What?'

'And His Excellency.' Fatima was genuinely shocked. 'They attacked him?' She sounded as if she could not believe it.

'No—'

But Fatima was plucking at the torn trousers, shaking her head, and Leo realised what she was talking about. She blushed.

'We, er, there was a bit of an accident,' she said lamely.

Fatima was horrified. 'You are hurt?'

To the heart, thought Leo.

'No,' she said.

Fatima was not convinced.

'You shall rest,' she said firmly. 'And then we will heat water and you shall bathe before you dine with His Excellency.'

They had set his own tent out as efficiently as ever. Even though he had left in such a hurry, his staff had followed with the full complement of equipment. The camp was now

the luxury resting place that they prepared when he and his
father went on hawking trips in the desert.

Amer unbuckled his dagger and sank wearily onto a divan.

What a damned thing to happen. He had thought he could
show her that he respected her. That he needed her. She already knew how much he wanted her, God help them both.
And then Saeed and his heroes had frightened her half to
death and he, Amer, had shouted at her and all but lost control in the terrifying rush of relief in knowing her safe.

She was not a trusting woman. Would she ever trust him
now?

Amer gave a mirthless laugh.

Fatima brought Leo a lemon sherbet. While Leo sipped at
the sharp, foaming drink, Fatima slipped her out of her ragged clothes and helped her into a cotton robe.

Leo saw that the tent had been prepared with care. The
ground was covered in rugs, one piled carelessly on the other,
worked in indigo and turquoise and a brilliant cornflower
blue that burned like the sun outside. On the top one there
was a design of the tree of life picked out in blood-red and
jet.

'That is a masterpiece,' she said, hesitating to walk on it.

Fatima smiled approvingly. 'It was Sheikh Amer who told
us to bring it. He said your tent had to be full of beautiful
things to distract you from ugliness.'

She magicked a director's chair from somewhere and disappeared.

Leo sank into the canvas seat and looked around. She
shook her head disbelievingly. She had not believed the comfort of her captors' tent. But that was as nothing to the sheer
luxury of this.

In addition to the amazing carpets, the main supports of
the tent were decorated with gauzy hangings on which there
was the distinct glint of gold motifs. A low divan was covered with midnight velvet and strewn with cushions in velvet
and brocade and shot silk in all the peacock colours: jade

and emerald and sea-green and navy. Again there was the glint of gold trimmings and tassels. Leo blinked at the gold but it looked blessedly comfortable.

'Just the thing for the Sultan's favourite,' she said ironically.

So why had Amer ordered this bower to be prepared for her? Did he expect to spend the night here? Her heart beat faster at the thought. And if he did, what was she going to do about it? Fall into his arms as she just had in the land cruiser? Or try to be sensible and guard her heart from another wounding power contest?

Guard her heart? Who was she trying to fool? What was the point of guarding something already utterly breached? Her heart was occupied territory now.

She submitted wearily to Fatima's ministrations. And fell into an exhausted sleep.

When she was awoke, the tent was almost in darkness. A small light burned steadily on a carved stool. Leo stretched slowly. Her dreams had been sensual in the extreme. She felt wonderful.

Fatima came in, her feet noiseless on the rich carpets.

'You are awake. Good. His Excellency said not to wake you.'

Leo frowned. 'Amer was here?'

Fatima's smile was bland.

'But *here*? Here in my tent?'

'He wanted to be sure that you had not taken any hurt from those villains. He watched over you while you slept.'

'Oh,' said Leo, shaken. 'I didn't know.'

But her body had known. And her dreams. She swallowed.

'His Excellency will dine with you,' Fatima informed her. 'So you will want to bathe, yes?'

Her tone implied *and make yourself beautiful for him*. The Sultan's favourite indeed, thought Leo, amused. But the idea was oddly exciting as well.

'Yes,' she agreed slowly. 'Yes, I will.'

Fatima helped Leo to her feet and led her tenderly through

the hangings. Leo was stunned. Set out for her pleasure was a hip bath of old-fashioned design. Steam and a delectable scent wafted up from it.

Two girls stood to one side. They carried pitchers half as big as they were and were trying hard to look solemn. Not very successfully.

Fatima frowned at them. She whipped away the loose robe in which Leo had slept and held her hand while she stepped gingerly into the bath. She gave her an enormous sponge that someone had dived into the depths of the Red Sea to bring back.

The girls looked agonized as they tried to control their excited giggles. At Fatima's command, they brought oils and shampoo and added warm water. It smelled of rose petals. She said so.

Fatima smiled. 'His Excellency's personal instruction,' she murmured.

Afterwards Fatima massaged Leo with scented oils until her muscles felt exquisitely toned. The girls stroked perfume into her wrists. Then they outlined her eyes with the finest possible trace of kohl and brushed her hair until it shone. They left it loose on her shoulders. Leo wondered if that was His Excellency's personal instruction as well. Finally they dressed her in silks so soft that her body hardly felt clothed.

Fatima gave her a mirror. Leo saw a woman she did not recognise: huge eyes, soft skin, vulnerable mouth. Too vulnerable? With sudden recklessness, Leo thought, *I'll take my chances*. She, who never trusted anyone! It was exhilarating.

Amer would not know her, she thought. Ah, but would he like her in this new guise? Leo gave a long sweet shiver of voluptuous anticipation. Over her shoulder Fatima smiled in complete female understanding.

'I will take you to Sheikh Amer,' she said.

Outside, the heat of the day had given place to a pleasant warmth. There was no breeze. On the other side of the camp Leo caught a glimpse of fires and heard cheerful voices.

Fatima skirted the main tent and took her to another, set a little away from the others.

'His Excellency's tent,' she explained.

For a moment Leo's courage almost deserted her. She hesitated, half wanting to turn back. But Fatima gave her a little push and disappeared.

Leo swallowed hard and went inside.

It was more austere than her tent but more magnificent. The divan was huge. There was an intricately carved desk, as well as chairs and several brass-bound trunks. The hangings and the rugs were sombre. But everywhere there was gold: trays, coffeepots, an oil lamp. Even Amer's curved dagger which lay discarded on the desk glinted with gold.

This is a dream, Leo thought. A deserted dream. She stopped hesitating and went, soft footed, to a gilt chair. She sat on the very edge of it, trying to be calm.

She was trying so hard that she did not hear Amer's step. He stood in the entrance for a moment, watching her bent head. He frowned.

'Are you all right?'

Leo jumped at the soft voice. She looked up quickly.

He seemed very tall. He was wearing black again, a loose coat in fine lawn, with a chased silver border, over a light robe. As he strode forward, she saw that he was wearing a deep belt of plaited leather decorated with beaten silver. He looked devastating.

'I'm f-fine.' But there was a catch in her voice.

'You don't sound very sure.'

Leo was briefly indignant. How could he expect her to be sure of anything? She was sitting here like a traditional plaything, bathed and scented for his pleasure. She did not feel like herself at all.

She almost said so. But the events of the day must have taken their toll. She could not face pointing out to Amer that she was cast as Harem Favourite and did not know the words because... Well, she just could not face it, that was all.

He was so distant, standing there. How could he be distant

after that crazy episode in the land cruiser? Was this the man who had flung himself upon her, shaking with passion?

Leo could not meet his eyes.

'I'm happy as a clam,' she said brusquely, her colour heightened.

Amer did not challenge her.

He said curtly, 'I said I wouldn't apologise. I was wrong. I'm sorry.'

Leo stared. Was he apologising for making her feel that he had wanted her? Really wanted her, without reservations? Or because he hadn't, in the end, wanted her enough. She felt as if he had hit her where she was most unguarded.

He added irritably, 'But you shouldn't have made me mad.'

Leo recovered. 'So it's my fault you attacked me?' she said, brutal in her hurt.

If he had really been sorry, she thought, he would have grovelled. He would have excused himself for being carried away by the strength of his feelings. He would have said he never meant to hurt her. He would have promised never to hurt her again. Never to take her to the very edge of Paradise and leave her there, abandoned.

He didn't. Instead he looked at her very levelly, not speaking. Leo felt her colour rise.

'What? What?' she said aggressively. 'I invited it? Is that what you mean? Well, is it?'

Oh where had all that lovely voluptuous expectation gone?

Amer said quietly, 'No more games, Leonora.'

'Games?' echoed Leo. She was outraged.

'Games.' He was sober. 'Be honest. We have both done our share of throwing down gauntlets. And I for one have enjoyed it. I admit it. But the time for all that is over.'

'Oh,' said Leo, disconcerted.

'When Saeed's group kidnapped you I felt—' He hesitated.

Leo held her breath.

'Responsible,' he finished.

The disappointment was so great that Leo could have wept.

She said in a hard voice, 'There's no need to feel responsible for me. If I hadn't chosen to go to the market against all advice, I would not have been kidnapped in the first place.'

Amer made an impatient gesture. 'That's not what I meant. I—'

They were interrupted by a courtly servant. Amer looked irritated. But he nodded.

'They have set a meal for us at the old excavations,' he said. 'I thought it would please you.'

Leo stood up obediently. Just for a moment Amer's face softened. He reached out and slid a hand under her hair. She could feel the warmth of his palm against her nape. It made her feel soft and shockingly vulnerable.

If only he loved me. The thought came out of nowhere. She bit her lip and retreated out of reach.

Amer's hand fell. His face lost all expression. He turned and led her out under the desert stars.

A rug had been set for them on the other side of the steps he had pointed out to her. They effectively screened them from the rest of the camp. Food was brought and placed on a wide cloth. They ate, though Leo had trouble swallowing even a mouthful. Eventually Amer waved the servants away.

Leo looked at the desert, stretching away to its meeting point with the stars. It was awe inspiring. In this sculpted wilderness the moon, she found, cast shadows. The stars blazed like a jeweller's tray of diamonds.

It made her feel tiny. She shivered.

Amer looked up. 'You are cold?'

'No.'

It was true. There was a breeze but it was warm, scented with strange desert grasses and wood smoke.

'You shivered.'

'Not from cold. This—' she gestured '—makes us seem very small, doesn't it? Just for a moment I felt really alone.'

'Alone? But I am here.'

In the dark Leo found the courage to say, 'But you haven't been very companionable.'

'Companionable!' He snorted contemptuously. 'What do you think I am, Leonora?' He sounded furious again.

She was confused. 'I don't understand.'

'Pets are companionable. Cats and little lap dogs are companionable. Like your Simon Hartley.'

'Simon?'

He smote one clenched hand into the other. 'Tell me now, Leonora. Were you really in love with that fool?'

Leo could not believe that he would ask. 'W-with Simon?' she said incredulously.

'When you broke off the engagement you said it was the worst day in your life,' he reminded her.

Leo had forgotten. She struggled to remember.

'Well, the *day* was. I had a mail-order ring and a journalist taking me to pieces. And that was before I found out that my engagement was a done deal between my father and an ambitious subordinate. How would you feel?'

Amer waited.

Leo cleared her throat. 'And then you were in town and I didn't understand you. I didn't know what you wanted.' She swallowed. 'I still don't.'

He made a disbelieving noise. 'Yet it is clear enough.'

'Not to me.'

'I want you,' he said in a matter-of-fact tone.

Leo sat utterly still. A little eddy of breeze lifted her hair from her lightly clad shoulders. She could not look at him.

She said sadly, 'Me? Or just not to lose the game?'

'What?' He was astounded.

Leo made a helpless gesture. '"Come with me to the Casbah",' she said.

'Oh not that again.' He made an impatient movement.

'No. Listen to me. It seemed to me that—' Heavens this was difficult '—that what happened between us was a sort of competitive game to you. I left Cairo and you couldn't find me. So I sort of won. And then—when I saw you in London—it seemed as if you had to get your own back.'

'What are you talking about?'

'The way you found out about me,' Leo said, trying to put the feeling into words. 'Picking me up in the limo when I wasn't expecting it. Carrying me off to dinner when I didn't want to go. It felt as if you were showing me you could do anything you liked with me.'

Which of course was true. But it *shouldn't* be true. And he certainly shouldn't be allowed to take advantage of it.

Amer let out an explosive breath. 'I told you. A man likes to do his own hunting.'

Leo shivered. 'Yes but I don't like feeling like quarry.'

He leaned forward suddenly, trying to make out her expression in the dark.

'Don't you?' Suddenly there was amusement in his voice.

Leo avoided his eyes and desperately looked for something to keep her hands busy. Or she would reach out to him. And that would be disastrous.

She took a peach she did not want. At once Amer took it from her and peeled it with a gold-handled knife. He had done that before, Leo remembered. She tried not to. His fingers were long and dextrous. Leo swallowed and avoided looking at his hands as well.

He said, 'What do you think has been happening here?'

That, thought Leo mutinously, is just not fair.

Aloud she said, 'I was stupid enough to challenge you at the Antika reception. You can't resist a challenge. Hence this nonsense about being engaged.'

'Nonsense?'

He passed her the neatly quartered peach. Leo looked at it and wondered how she was going to swallow a mouthful of it.

'Well, joke then,' she amended.

'In that case the joke has got a little out of hand, wouldn't you say?'

That hurt.

'Probably.' Leo replied. 'I'd better go home.'

'Running away again,' he said softly.

'I'm not running. I have a life to get on with.'

'Do you think I haven't?' he said on a flash of sudden anger. 'Dear Heaven, do you know how delicate the situation here is? How hard we have to work to keep it in equilibrium? Why the hell do you think I did not come to you on the one night you had eventually decided to accept me? I was with the Council, God help me, trying to stop my father starting a small war!'

Leo blinked at the suppressed fury in his tones. He banged his hand down on the cloth so hard that the little gold-stemmed goblets jumped. One fell over.

Leo forgot that it was dangerous to look him in the eye. Her head reared up, startled. Their eyes locked. Amer gave an odd laugh under his breath.

'This is getting us nowhere.'

He stood up and held out an imperious hand. 'Walk with me.'

Leo got to her feet. She knew it was not sensible. But she gave him her hand anyway. His fingers closed over hers. It seemed as if she felt his strength flow through her.

The warm desert night was heady, too heady. The vaulting sky was so bright and clear that it looked as if you could touch it. Leo staggered a little, feeling the world wheel.

Amer dropped her hand and put his arm round her. The world did not steady, but she leaned against him involuntarily. It made her feel safe and yet unsafe. As if he would protect her from every threat but himself. Who was the greatest threat of all.

Leo felt the chill of excitement touch her skin like the desert breeze.

He walked her purposefully towards a thin tree on the edge of the site.

'This was an iron age village,' he was saying. 'We think they brought water from the mountains by means of underground pipes. We have found the access shaft here, we think.

But we don't know which direction the water came from, yet.'

Against her, his shoulder felt like a rock. Warm rock.

'H-how interesting,' Leo managed to say.

'There was a time,' Amer said very deliberately, 'as I mentioned to you before, when I thought I would be an archaeologist. My father has the right to chose his heir and he and I did not see eye to eye at all. I thought he would choose one of my uncles. Very traditional, very unyielding. To be honest I would have been glad. But the last three years he has been wavering. Now he says he sees that reform is necessary and I am the one to do it.' He sighed. 'So my water pipes will be discovered by somebody else.'

He paused, as if he expected a reaction.

Bewildered, Leo said, 'Why are you telling me this?'

The arm around her was like iron.

'Because I want you to know me,' Amer said simply.

She levered herself away a little and stared up at him. The moonlight hid his expression. She gave a cynical nod.

'Oh, sure.'

He was startled. 'What do you mean?'

'If you wanted me to know you, could you have told me about your wife,' Leo said before she could stop herself.

'My wife!' He sounded thunderstruck.

'If there was anything more to this than a sexy game of pursuit, wouldn't you have told me that at least?' Leo said quietly.

There was a silence.

Then Amer said fiercely, 'My feelings for my wife were nothing like this. *Nothing*.'

Leo thought it was impossible to hurt so much and not cry out with it. She removed herself from his encircling arm. She could not bear him to touch her any more and not *care*.

She said, 'I want to go back.'

'Leonora—'

'I want to go back *now*.'

She fled.

He let her get as far as their picnic site before he caught her. His arms shackled her, though she struggled wildly.

'Let me go,' she panted. 'You don't want me. Not really. For a few days at most.'

'A few days?' Amer speared a look down into her face that she could almost believe would pierce the dark. 'A few *days?*'

He pulled her hard into his arms. Leo suddenly saw the point of light, loose silks. His head blotted out the moon.

It was no good. No matter what her head said, her heart was his. She gave herself up to the moment on a tornado of desire.

He lowered her to the rug. The sand shifted underneath, moulding itself round them. Leo gasped. His hands were strong and amazingly competent. She felt the silks flow away from her. To be replaced by his mouth.

But this was not like London. This was no languorous lovemaking, luring her slowly up the winding path of pleasure. This was urgent. Desperate almost. And this time he was not holding back.

'Touch me,' he commanded.

Leo hesitated. He groaned her name. She had never felt so unsure of herself. His flesh was so warm. Tentatively she moved her palms along his shoulder, down his spine. It felt awkward. His tension struck her to the heart.

It was no use. She could not pretend.

With harsh honesty, Leo said, 'I don't know how to do this.'

Amer raised his head at that. 'What?'

In the starlight his eyes burned into hers.

Leo had no deceptions left. 'No one has ever made me feel the way you do,' she muttered. 'I didn't know anyone could. I have no idea how to make you feel that good. I've always been useless with men.'

She felt as if her whole body was one huge blush of shame. Thank God for the dark. At least he would not see it.

See? No. But he could hear. And feel. He was very still

for an agonizing moment. Then he moved sharply, pinning her hands above her head in the sand.

'And you accused *me* of treating this like a game,' he said, outraged.

Leo was disconcerted. She pulled against the imprisoning hands. 'What? What are you doing?'

But he did not let her go. It was almost as if he did not hear her. She started to thresh wildly.

'You're not a toy,' he said furiously. 'That's why I went after you in the first place. You were completely yourself.'

Leo tried to kick herself free. It was an incredible mistake. His hand only tightened on her wrist. But the worst thing was that it brought her into contact with the whole length of his aroused body. She sobbed in longing.

'You don't have to make me feel good.' Amer shook her wrists to emphasise his point. 'You don't have to make me feel *anything*. You have to be here. That's all. Be here now.'

'Let me go,' said Leo breathlessly.

Her writhings had taken them off the rug into the sand.

'Feel,' he said. 'Just feel.'

You have to be here. Now.

His concentration was total. It was like fire. She cried out again and again as he swept through defence after defence to reach the heated core of her.

You have to be. Here. *Now*.

Leo lay stunned. Her unwinking eyes gazed dreamily at the stars, wheeling with majestic slowness beyond his head. He was heavy across her, his forehead damp in the crook of her shoulder. She touched his hair with tenderness. And absolute love.

It did not matter if he did not love her. It did not matter how short a time he might want her for. She loved him. And he had loved her in a way for that explosive moment.

Amer stirred.

'I never meant to do that,' he said. His voice was slurred but there was an unmistakable undertone of laughter. 'Well not yet anyway. You go to my head.'

He rolled away and sat up. Leo lay there in the starlight, unashamed of her nakedness, though she knew he was looking at her. She gazed up at him with love.

He brushed her hair back from her hot face. It was a possessive gesture.

'I hurt you, didn't I?'

'No.'

'I think I did.'

Leo stretched her arms above her head. She gave her limbs a shake all the way down to her pointing toes. She made a little purring sound.

'No,' she said, laughing in her turn. 'All in good working order. In fact, this is the best I've ever felt in my life.'

Amer bent and kissed her quickly. 'Me, too.'

'You?' She came up on one elbow, astonished. 'But—'

He said rapidly, 'I know I should have told you about Yasmin. Only it's painful. I've got out of the way of thinking about it.'

Leo leaned forward and put a hand to his cheek.

'Yasmin was your wife?'

For some reason it did not seem all that important, any more. She loved him. That was enough.

'Yes. We were too young, I suppose. And it was a political alliance. She had been spoilt by her father. I was too young to know how to deal with it. It made her cruel.' He looked into Leo's eyes suddenly. 'When she died she was tormenting a horse she had been told she should not ride. I couldn't mourn. I couldn't forgive myself for not mourning. It's a bad package, that.'

Leo pulled him forward until his head was against her breast.

'Oh my love.'

'I'm not proud of the way I've lived since then. I wish it had been different. That's why I held back that night in London. I wanted—it seemed a way of loving you.'

Leo's eyes were full of tears. She bent her head quickly to kiss his temple. Her lips trembled.

'I have never wanted any woman to have my children,' he said so quietly that she could barely hear him. 'Until now.'

Leo went very still. Amer raised his head.

'That's why no more games.' He stroked her hair. 'It's a lot of fun and sexy as hell. But I want more.'

She was utterly unprepared. 'I can't—I hadn't thought—I didn't know—' She swallowed. 'But you don't love me.'

'Don't I?'

'You haven't shown any signs of it.'

Amer gave a tender laugh. 'That's because you don't know what a saint I normally am. Hari tells me I've been unbearable. And doing crazy things, just for the chance of getting you into bed.'

'Oh,' said Leo, hopefully.

'My father could tell you, too,' Amer added thoughtfully. 'I said that unless he agreed to meet you I was going to take up an archaeological job in the UK.'

'*Oh.*'

'Marry me,' he said urgently.

Leo blinked, disconcerted.

'All right,' he said in a reasonable voice. 'Spend the night with me. We'll talk about the rest in the morning.'

Leo was startled into laughter. Amazed, joyous laughter.

'But I'm clumsy. And I bump into things. And I get ink on my fingers. What sort of wife will I make?'

'The only one I want.'

Amer kissed her throat. 'Are you going to spend the night with me or not, you difficult woman?'

Leo moved against him voluptuously, her eyes drifting shut.

'I'll take that as a yes,' said Amer amused. 'And what about marriage?'

Amused, yes. But he was shaking. He wanted her. He really wanted her!

Leo opened her eyes and gave him a long look of shameless triumph.

'Yes,' she said.

EPILOGUE

IT WAS, everyone agreed, a magnificent wedding. It went on for four days and included every ceremony that the bride's and groom's respective families could devise.

After the ceremonies came the feasting; after the feasting the entertainment. The Minister of Culture, in his element, hung the palace halls with cloth of gold for the occasion. The international photojournalists were in their element.

Leo went through it all without bumping into a thing. Every time she felt nervous she looked up. And Amer smiled at her as if he and she were the only people in the world.

Eventually she slipped away from the music and dancing and out into the courtyard where the fountains played. He followed her, as she knew he would.

'Tired?' The soft murmur was a caress.

'No.'

'So you would like to dance until dawn?' he teased.

'No.'

'So what am I to do with you, then?'

'Love me.'

His arms closed round her, hard as iron. 'Always.'

'Take me home, Amer.' Her voice was a thread of pure desire.

He took her back to his own palace then; to his private room, with its books and the mountains beyond. And shut the world out.

Leo gave a little delighted shiver and went into his arms in total trust.

'It seems too much. I can't believe it. Hold me, my love. Make me believe it.'

'Believe what?' he said, his voice husky with desire. 'That

185

I adore you? That when I am away from you, I can barely wait to return to you? That when I return, all I want is you in my arms?'

Leo was trembling. 'That I am the Sheikh's bride, after all.'

He picked her up and carried her to the bed.

And in the end, dazed with delight, humbled by love and completely overthrown by tender laughter, she said, 'I believe it. Oh boy, do I believe.'

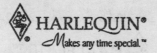

Harlequin Romance®

Experience the ultimate desert fantasy with this thrilling new Sheikh miniseries!

Four best-loved Harlequin Romance® authors bring you strong, proud Arabian men, exotic eastern settings and plenty of tender passion under the hot desert sun....

Look out for:

His Desert Rose by Liz Fielding
(#3618) in August 2000

To Marry a Sheikh by Day Leclaire
(#3623) in October 2000

The Sheikh's Bride by Sophie Weston
(#3630) in November 2000

The Sheikh's Reward by Lucy Gordon
(#3634) in December 2000

Available in August, September, October and November wherever Harlequin Books are sold.

CELEBRATE VALENTINE'S DAY WITH HARLEQUIN®'S LATEST TITLE— Stolen Memories

Available in trade-size format, this collector's edition contains three full-length novels by *New York Times* bestselling authors Jayne Ann Krentz and Tess Gerritsen, along with national bestselling author Stella Cameron.

TEST OF TIME by Jayne Ann Krentz—
He married for the best reason.... She married for the only reason.... Did they stand a chance at making the only reason the real reason to share a lifetime?

THIEF OF HEARTS by Tess Gerritsen—
Their distrust of each other was only as strong as their desire. And Jordan began to fear that Diana was more than just a thief of hearts.

MOONTIDE by Stella Cameron—
For Andrew, Greer's return is a miracle. It had broken his heart to let her go. Now fate has brought them back together. And he won't lose her again...

Make this Valentine's Day one to remember!

Look for this exciting collector's edition on sale January 2001 at your favorite retail outlet.

HARLEQUIN®
Makes any time special ™